THE GARDEN

OF DEPARTED

CATS

To Kitty, Margo, Zelda and, of course, Phoebe

—A.A.

THE GARDEN OF DEPARTED CATS

BILGE KARASU

Translated from the Turkish by Aron Aji

A NEW DIRECTIONS PAPERBOOK ORIGINAL

Originally published in Turkey by Metis Yayinlari as GÖÇMÜS KEDILER
BAHÇESI in 1991.

Published by arrangement with Metis Yayinlari.

Grateful acknowledgments are made to the editors and publisher of GRAND
STREET, in which "Hurt Me Not," the ninth tale of this book, was first
published.

Manufactured in the United States of America.
New Directions Books are printed on acid-free paper.
First published as a New Directions Paperbook(NDP965) in 2003.
Published simultaneously in Canada by Penguin Books Canada Limited.
Design by Semadar Megged.

Library of Congress Cataloging-in-Publication Data

Karasu, Bilge.
  [Gèo<eth>cmèu<eth>s kediler bahcesi English]
  The garden of departed cats / Bilge Karasu ; translated from the
Turkish by Aron Aji.
      p. cm.
Originally published under title: Gèo<eth>cmèu<eth>s kediler bah<eth>cesi.
Turkey :
Metis Yay,nlar,, 1991.
  ISBN 0-8112-1551-2
  I. Aji, Aron, 1960- II. Title.
  PL248.K33G6313 2003
  894'.3533—dc21

                              2003013221

New Directions Books are published for James Laughlin
by New Directions Publishing Corporation
80 Eighth Avenue, New York 10011

CONTENTS

THE GARDEN

OF DEPARTED

CATS

The truest fairy tale is the one we are afraid to understand.
                                        —*Talat Halman*

THE GARDEN OF DEPARTED CATS

To Enis

*Entre vos mains mêmes, ces êtres-là
son des êtres de fuite.*
—*M. Proust*

1.

I arrived one afternoon in the medieval city located in the center of this narrow peninsula that stretches like an arm into the Mediterranean. For forty days, I had been shuttling east and west, north and south, in an area barely two hundred miles square. I had visited about twenty cities, big and small, cities still bearing the pride of the sovereign states they'd once been. Most were located along rivers or in valleys, although some perched on steep rocky cliffs, and in others, the sea breeze would carry salt into the streets. . . .

I would spend a day or two visiting each city, and take an evening train to the next one an hour or so away. With each passing day, more and more feeling the fatigue of my travels, I constantly was devising new ways to fight my exhaustion so I could find the strength to go out and eat at least and, perhaps, see a movie afterwards, if the film interested me.

Autumn had settled in; yet the trees seemed unchanged, except that, in the breeze, their rustling was more poignant. Even the fruit trees bore no sign of fading, drying or shedding their leaves. In this poplar country, the pine trees were a crowded minority.

The sun hadn't yet set when I arrived in this land-locked city proud of its enduring medieval character. It covered one side of a hill; at its peak stood the cathedral that I planned to visit the next day. At first glance, I couldn't decide if the lofty building was taller or wider. It had to be quite large.

Halfway down the hill was a hotel built to resemble an ancient inn. In my room, the water from the faucet was warm at first so I began washing; I kept splashing my body even when the water got cold. Then I slept. In less than an hour, I got up feeling refreshed, as if I had a long restful sleep, and I went out to eat.

There were three other people in the restaurant, each sitting at a separate table. Two had their faces toward me, one his back. While waiting to be served, I looked past the two faces and focused my attention on the third man, expecting him to turn and face me. Meanwhile, I was trying out in my notebook sentences for a narrative that was slowly coming into being.

My meal lasted an hour and a half. The waiter and the cook were slow and I was in no particular hurry. The cinema was just across the narrow main street, just steps from where I sat. The film started at nine o'clock. I had plenty of time to walk to the sweet shop, only six steps from the cinema, and buy some of the famous sweets of the medieval festivals.

In this hour and a half, the two men whose faces I could see stood up and left, three others arrived and sat. When they ordered their food, I asked for my bill.

But I had yet to see the face of the man with his back turned to me. He also seemed to be writing something. Perhaps a letter or an essay. I tore off the notebook pages that had the eight sentences I would later transfer to my draft book. I put those pages in my pocket and on the remaining page, I jotted down, just for the sake of jotting, the words, "In The Garden of the Departed, A Summer Romance," and I thought of leaving the page on the table, wondering whether the waiter would notice it and try to *decode this scribbling in a strange language, whether he would run after me, calling me. Instead, I crumpled the page and pitched it in the ashtray.*

We got up at the same time. Our eyes met. I felt a dizzy spell in my head, a reverberation. He walked past me. Ten steps between us, we walked to the sweet shop, then to the cinema. I couldn't see him after the film. At the hotel entrance, we met again, paused momentarily, exchanged abrupt "after-you-no-after-you's." In the landing on the first floor, he stopped briefly when I turned to walk toward my room; he then walked behind me, opened the door facing mine, and went inside.

"I am the sea teeming with sunken loves."
—*M. C. Anday*

THE PREY

To the Açars

I'm torn between a sunny winter day that faintly prom-
ises summer, and the one four days later, a day of snow,
blizzard, with two feet accumulating. I can't decide
which day to choose for my tale.

I'm also thinking this:

Love means—literally or figuratively—eating and nothing else. . . .

The sea: it will either become a mirror under the winter sun, or its tall jagged waves will rush and recede in the
blizzard that turns day into night.

The sea must always come first. Because it holds the
fish and the fisherman. Because its myriad fingers sweep
the fish and the fisherman, wherever it wishes, now smiling on the fish now on the fisherman, now disappointing
one now the other.

The fish comes next: it is an intermediary between the
sea and the fisherman. The fish perceives the fisherman as
the enemy, and doesn't know that the sea, which holds
them both, will use one to lure the other. The fish. If the

day is sunny, the fish will exhaust the fisherman. If snowy, it will rise to the surface, numb, overwhelmed by the cold.

At last the fisherman: he knows nothing besides the sea's annihilation or the bends. He will come to know love—if he ever does—through the fish. Human. . . .

Suppose we choose the sunny day (perhaps also to please the most readers). Suppose the fisherman sails off, say, when the currents move gently, almost without a ripple, between the coast and the islands . . . Most often, the sea favors the fisherman. Yet when his journey proves plentiful, he credits himself, his good fortune, his skills. The sea knows well what humans refuse to understand, that what they deem obvious the sea knows is unintelligible. The one who knows remains silent.

And one more thing:

The sea loves this fisherman. It is the kind of love humans wrongly call "hopeless."

Since the mind cannot even begin to fathom the love offered by an immeasurably vast sea, the fisherman responds to it in the only way he can: he is satisfied that the sea is his livelihood (and in due time, his death bed). To the outsider, everything appears crystal clear. Yet something is overlooked: the insider is inside and sees only what's inside.

(Besides, don't we know? People are outraged that one can commit murder in the name of love and they heap curse upon curse on the murderer. Then, one day, the same people are seized by the realization that they are just as capable of murdering in the name of love, that in their hearts they have already rehearsed the horrid act, already felt it in the depths of their being. Then it is someone else's turn to curse . . .)

Between the coast and the islands, the gentle currents will carry the fisherman to the spot where a young misguided fish will be circling greedily. The fish will catch the bait effortlessly, then fight the line with all its strength, fight and wear down the fisherman. When the fish is defeated at last and is being pulled into the boat, the fisherman's arm . . .

In the struggle with the fish—that is like no other fish he has known or caught—he will be exhausted. . . . In a way, what happens afterwards will be his reward . . .

Or if the events happen on the day of the blizzard, then the sea will exhaust both the fish and the fisherman. People usually value something obtained after much struggle. Some believe they catch the difficult bounty with the strength of their arm, with their intelligence. Yet, others have subtler interests: they neither care for easy achievement nor enjoy being perceived as chasing what they desire; therefore, even in the most difficult circumstances, they feign indifference and wait instead for the prey—the object of their desire, or their chase—to give up the chase and surrender. Then their satisfaction is even greater. Could there be a prey this heedless? Absolutely.

The sea will assume a color between lead and olive, enduring turmoil between periods of hailstorm. In a few hours, the annihilation will start. The shores, the boats along the shores, will be covered in snow. The icy currents will flow into underwater shelters where schools of fish retreat. Numbed, the fish will gradually be overwhelmed by the cold, rise to the surface, half dead, and succumb to the currents. Later, they will be swept ashore, filling the scoops and buckets of those who may enjoy a difficult chase but won't turn down easy prey.

• • •

The startled horse sprang forward. Falcons, lances, maces came flying behind the horseman. The Bey rode swiftly toward the rocky cliffs, chasing the deer, the leopard, the mountain goat.

• • •

Annihilation is still a few hours ahead of him. The fish
that he hopes will come to him—although it never has,
not even once—must be lost, inexperienced, a naïve creature. It doesn't yet know the snow, the numbness, the annihilation that the cold weather brings. It mustn't know.

So that, while the fish is being pulled into the boat, the
fisherman's arm . . .

Or we may suppose altogether differently and com-
bine the two weathers. Say the sea is pale, the sky icy gray,
the morning snow has stopped, and the sunlight is seeping
through the folds of gray. Gathering snow, so to speak. Yet
even so little sunlight suffices to warm the human heart,
the veins that have grown thin, atrophied; it provides a
faint reassurance that everything need not die in the cold,
even knowing that the warmth will be brief, that the snow
and the annihilation are about to start. . . .

The fisherman pulls the line, his hand is covered with
blood. He can sense the beauty of the fish, the sweet teasing in his heart.

• • •

This is not a fairy-tale horse. It lies on the ground, mutilated. The Bey rests his weight on his lance and stares at
the beast. The leopard's head is soaked in blood. How
could he have loved this leopard?

• • •

This immense, this magnificent fish, if it caught the hook,
it probably wasn't because its palate was itching. When
reeled in, the fish had its mouth open, as if to show where
the hook tore through the skin, asking to be taken gently,
unharmed. The fisherman did what he should never have
done: he wrapped his right arm around the fish, pressed
the creature to his body, and, in this embrace, he put his
left hand inside the mouth to remove the hook carefully.

The mouth closed shut. He felt the hook sliding across his hand, his wrist, his arm. He couldn't free his hand, and his arm slowly began disappearing inside the mouth. He felt no pain. His arm wasn't being bitten or torn; it was merely being swallowed. The fish stopped at his elbow. Without struggle, it stared at him with one enormous eye. The fish just hung on to his arm.

The fisherman managed to gather himself together somehow. First he tried to pull out of the fish gently but he couldn't even move it. When he tightened his grip, he felt the spikes and sharp scales throughout the animal's startled skin; his right hand was scraped all over, covered in blood. When he tried to open the jaws, he felt the teeth piercing his flesh. He stopped. He needed to think and act at once. He began to row with his free arm, even though he knew the act was futile. Soon he noticed that he was caught in a current. He pulled out the oar and surrendered to the movement.

Someone in the distance, somewhere deep in the water, was teasing him, laughing at him. So it seemed to him.

• • •

A fish inside the sea's darkness; a snake inside the earth's darkness. Messengers from the dead.

A fish disappears in the brilliance of the sky. Or is it a seagull? Perhaps. A messenger from the resurrected. What counsel does it bring to us? To the fisherman above whose head it glides?

Behind a mound are men in turbans and hoods; they look at the Bey, as if spying on him.

A snake lays coiled by a tree, in its shade. Little farther, the same snake—it must be—slithers to its hole. Does it portend the Bey's killing of the leopard? or his imminent death?

A creek below; in the creek, a gliding fish.

From behind the mound, an arrow shoots toward the Bey. Above him, among the tree branches, a bird stretches its wings, prepares to soar into the brilliant void.

• • •

From now on, the fish is his burden. He can neither sail nor row, nor even walk among the people. He cannot bring himself to kill the fish. How can he? What instrument can he use?

He remembers something from the drowsy past, vaguely stirring. . . .

A boy is running the length of a sandy shore. He is holding a snake by its neck. The snake doesn't resist, it simply administers the child his punishment: swinging its entire body like a flaming whip, it bloodies his arm, wrist and hand. The boy catches up with his brother, shows him the snake, slowly squeezes its neck one last time then releases it. The snake slithers, disappearing from sight like a flash of lightning. Without harming the boy. It has punished him enough. The smile doesn't leave the boy's face even for a moment. "Where did you find it?" "In the sand." "How did you catch it?" "In a snap, grabbed it by its neck." Much later he recites, as if by heart, "We are friends now."

This is what he remembers. From the past, through the vaguely stirring darkness of its drowsy waters.

"We are friends now," he repeats—feeling his voice inside his throat more than hearing it—as if to commit it to heart: "We are friends now." The fish doesn't move, gazing at his face with one enormous eye. Even after many hours out of the water, the fish is indistinguishable from any land creature. One could almost say it breathes, almost notice the breathing.

Who is the prey? the fish or the fisherman? Perhaps each has surrendered to the other in the mysterious hunt.

"We are friends now." The fish wants more than

friendship, it is obvious. As the hours pass, what is between them will be love, will turn into passion. It is already love, already turning into passion . . .

• • •

Arrows come flying. They fall under the Tree of Eternity and become blades of grass. The shoots are the arrows that fall like rain—or the rain that falls like arrows. Among the blades, a snake uncoils, both male and female.

The Sacred Tree, the Tree of Eternity, is the mainmast of the universe. Kings camp under it and pour libations at its roots. They strangle the lion and the leopard between their arms and chest, snatch the last breath out of them with one hand. They tear wild beasts in two, grabbing them now by their jaws now by their hind legs, and choke the snake that wraps around their legs. The world belongs to the kings. The Tree grants them strength. Because they don't know love, they enrage the Matriarch of animals, and yet, by pouring their libations that seep into the soil, they rejoin husbands and wives, lost lovers. The kings stand by the tree, as if holding together the universe: the sky is above them, the earth is their body, the underground streams carry their feet. Because their bodies are one with the Tree, their heads dwell among the birds, their feet among the fish.

• • •

The fisherman is inside the dream of a different kind of sleep. He no longer feels the weight on his arm. It's as though the fish has somehow released his arm only to swallow his entire body. Whether his head is still visible or it has become one with the fish's head, no one can tell.

Inside the fish and one with the fish, he leaves—whether leaving his room or his boat, this, too, no one can tell—and descends into the darkness of the cold currents. Night. The snow has stopped. The sun that once comforted the heart is extinguished. The two of them journey to the very depths, to a place that is eternally male, eternally female.

In the wake of the annihilation, the numbed fish begin their slow and fatal ascent to the icy surface, while the two, one inside the other, dive down among the colors, among the dead—new and ancient—bathed in strange brilliance, amid the ruins of sunken cities. The fisherman is not afraid of the colors, the brilliance, the moss-covered dead, or the petrified structures; he seems ready to feast on all shades of green. *As long*, he thinks, *as long as*, he says, hoping, knowing the fish also will understand him, *as long as*, he thinks and says, *I don't come face to face with the sultan of death. I'm not ready for that.*

But the fish doesn't seem to understand or know any of this. Its tail touches the rock at the end of their journey. The rock begins to split in two. He knows that only those who have befriended the snake and spoken to the seagull can enter through this narrow opening to kneel down and press their cheek against the feet of death. They alone can postpone the dark prince's ascent to earth. If they're not quick enough to go in, the crack closes, never to open again. Then, human hope is lost forever.

The fisherman repeats, "I am not ready." The outcome of this encounter is always uncertain; one can emerge from the darkness and return to earth, having learned something; or one may never emerge, never return. . . .

"I am not ready," he says; he escapes by sacrificing the part of his fin caught between the closing halves of the rock. His pain is unbearable. Again, he feels the weight around his arm, becomes conscious of his torn flesh where the hook had pierced it, and he awakens. The torn fin that is bleeding belongs to the fish. A tear forms in the corner of his eye.

Perhaps the boat is still riding the currents above, in the distance above . . . The two begin to rise like the throngs of devastated fish, streaks of tears and blood marking their ascent. Then, "The bends," he says, "the bends, I should have known," he thinks—he finds the time to think—perhaps. . . . Without realizing that it is the sea that has struck him.

• • •

Once, he thought that he and the snake had become friends, equals. He had captured the snake, and the snake had punished him for its captivity. After that, neither one had attempted to harm the other. Yet, because the fish wanted something beyond friendship, it swallowed his arm inch by inch, all the way up to his shoulder. As it swallowed, the fish grew bigger, heavier.

While the fish grew heavier, the fisherman came to realize that he loved this weight which was making his heart feel lighter. Although he felt cold, an inner flame was warming him and the fish. Little by little, he began to understand the language of the fish. Who knows, perhaps it was the fish that began to understand the language of the fisherman. Either way, they gradually came to understand each other.

"Go back to sleep," the fish told him. "We failed to enter the darkness because you said you weren't ready; you were afraid of death. Yet, unless you enter, unless you feel the pain of being torn to pieces, your heart cannot be renewed, you cannot be reborn."

"I would go anywhere with you," answered the fisherman. "But, if I'm not ready, what's the point of going, even with you?" The words he spoke didn't even persuade his own heart.

• • •

The boy brings his first prey and lays it before the elders. He waits, his eyes staring at the ground. The patriarch of the clan cuts the animal open, takes from its blood and smears it in nine places on the boy's body. With his skilled hands, he strips the most beautiful bone off the animal's right leg and gives it to the boy. "From now on, everyone will know you by the name I give you," he says. "Your name . . ." At that moment, the sky roars with thunder. The boy remains nameless.

For a long time, the fisherman cannot tell whether he is under the water or above it, whether on the surface or at the bottom. He is searching for a name, perhaps for himself, perhaps for the fish, or perhaps for the creature formed out of the two. As though surrounded by mirrors that multiply endlessly, he looks, he sees, and the more he looks the more he sees: one, a hundred, a thousand creatures that he has never seen before. A man whose arm is the body of a fish; a fish whose mouth holds a human head; a man swallowed by a fish; a fish and a man coupling; a man who is a fish who is a man; a fish, a man, self-coupling . . . Endlessly. One, a hundred, a thousand, still thousands of creatures that coil and tremble, uncoil and swell with maddening pleasure; a creature born out of a singular drunkenness, reborn into eternity, a creature engendered by pleasure. Endlessly.

Besides, he has seen fish couple only in pictures drawn merely for idle play.

It is as though someone is whispering the name he has been searching for, but the fisherman doesn't hear it. He cannot make out the name being whispered.

The sky brightens every now and then. Perhaps the sun keeps rising and setting; perhaps the clouds break and separate. One thing he knows is this brilliance, its intensity.

He tries to think: I went out fishing and returned inside my prey. He knows he is speaking nonsense. This is not my prey, he says; neither did I chase it nor was it caught; ours was a fortuitous encounter. We aren't altogether inside one another either: we became whatever the fish wants, however the fish wants it . . . Besides, have I even returned? Where? To whom? When have I returned? I am on a strange path, an uncommon journey. It is true, I am forced to live together with the fish, the creature that made me catch it and then swallowed me. Why am I talking like this? Don't I enjoy this union? We are inseparable, and this is all that can be said, all that is certain. Nothing else.

He gives up thinking. Because now they are rising toward daylight.

There is no light, no shimmers in the water. It's as if they are inside a milky way, far from the earth. "We both must have died," the fisherman thinks or the thought takes hold of the fisherman. "I still bear its weight, yet I feel as if we are gliding."

They are dead, torn to pieces; their hearts, their spleens, their bowels are renewed perhaps; perhaps they are reborn . . .

The dead know everything. Dying is the path to knowing. The one who dies and disappears among the dead, who descends into the underground or the underwater, and receives their advice; the one who ascends to the sky and beyond, who gathers light, enlightenment, wisdom—as if gathering flowers; the one who restores his mutilated body, brings about his own renewal, rebirth, and who returns to the earth to mix among the living, he is the one who knows everything worth knowing.

I have died, I shall be reborn and all-knowing, the fisherman says.

The fish thrusts its teeth into his shoulder. He mustn't forget the fish. He mustn't be overcome with pride.

Above them, a seagull spreads its wings like the crown of a tree. The fisherman is the trunk of that tree. The fish is inseparable from his shoulder, but its body extends into the distance—like the face of the earth or the sea. The sky, the earth, the deep water seem to have united in this Tree of Eternity. They have become, as it were, the entire universe. The fisherman knows that the fish is attached to him; what he sees below him is the sea. Until now, he had not seen the sea since he had been thinking through the mind of the fish. Then, suddenly—

A humming sound in the distance—it's been approaching for some time, yet still is in the distance. Suddenly, it surges, a blast in his ear. That is how he experiences it. As the fisherman and the fish begin falling at a blinding speed, the seagull falling with them, he sees the sea spreading itself out, opening its myriad fingers below them, and he feels the fish tightening its grip around his arm, with all the force it can muster. Then darkness surrounds them.

• • •

The Bey rode his horse like a flash of light, chasing the deer. The horse spread its wings, its shadow almost touching the deer. The prey stopped suddenly, as if turned to stone. Worlds collided in this mad pursuit. The Bey lay on the ground, his neck broken, his face covered in blood. Who would have known that the one who tried to revive him with tears was a young man with long hair, long fingers, a beauty among beauties, standing in the place of the elusive deer? Who would have explained it afterwards?

The unicorn is fond of virgins. The fabled creature runs and throws himself into her embrace, laying its head on her lap: Everybody knows this. And the only way to capture a unicorn and display heroism is by dressing a handsome young man as a maiden and setting him out on the meadow. The young man walks coquettishly; the unicorn sees him, comes running, throws himself into the young man's embrace. Then the lances hidden under the folds of gowns are revealed and the unicorn's chest is pierced in a hundred places.

• • •

People yearn to return to paradise, its vague memory lodged in a remote corner of their minds. But how many manage to recover even a piece of that paradise? Perhaps it would have been possible in the past, the very ancient past. Nowadays, to believe in returning to paradise no longer means believing that everything devastated begins anew, or that a dying year ushers in a new one. People don't believe they can die and be reborn time after time. In the tedious flow of existence, how many might be aware, for instance, that carrying the fish that swallowed one's arm is a proof of wisdom, of attainment? Even before anyone else might understand, the one whose arm the fish has swallowed views the fish as a badge not of wisdom but of hopeless love. He looks to find virtue in the painful endurance, in having surrendered to relentless annihilation.

The fisherman sees himself among his friends, sitting in a coffee house. They surround him; he sees grief in their faces. They obviously notice neither the fish nor his arm inside the fish. They ask where he has been for days, they tell him they were worried he'd had an accident. No one asks how he has lost his arm. And not without good reason either . . . If a man were to lose his arm, he couldn't recover in a few days. Besides, if he'd had an accident, they would have heard, or if he'd been in the hospital, they would have known. Not a word escapes the fisherman's lips. Only, he is sorry that no one can see the fish. And, why lie about this: he wants to shout at them, to ask why they don't see the immense fish that has swallowed his arm, but he cannot find the courage. Why should the act of making others see his beloved require so much heart, such a show of bravery, when he in fact already wants to flaunt his love? He returns home disgusted with himself. Yes, now he sees himself at home. As if he weren't the one who had descended into the deep or soared into the sky with the fish. He senses the fish throughout his

being, as if it has swallowed him completely. They didn't
see you, couldn't see you, he says, in a defeated voice.
What should I do to make them see you? Talk to them?
Explain? They'd say I was crazy. Perhaps let them touch
you? Can they touch a fish in place of the arm they cannot
see? To tell you the truth, I can't take the chance. Perhaps
now I understand, now I know, I cannot do without you.
Perhaps this is what I fear: that they may take you away
from me. He pauses. For the first time, he is able to think,
and speak out such thoughts. For the first time, love assumes the shape of his own words. I will go anywhere with
you, even there: to death's kingdom at the bottom of the
sea . . . I am ready, now I'm ready, we can even go to
death . . .

Suddenly he sees himself in his boat. Under a lead-
colored sky soon to turn pitch black. The boat is still riding the currents. The weight on his arm feels lighter. At
first, he thinks it is because his love is strong, but soon he
realizes that the fish is withering away as it dries out, its
flesh breaking open as it rots. Its teeth still pierce his
shoulder, even though the fish is rapidly decomposing,
turning into a cage of bones. The fisherman thinks he is
going mad—that is, if he hasn't already. He doesn't understand, doesn't want to understand. As the fish decays and
crumbles, it consumes his own flesh, and his bones begin
to show, and then to crumble like those of the fish. His
upper arm dissolves, and the remains of the fish's head dis-
solve, and that's when the fisherman decides what he must
do. He turns his boat around, facing the shore, and lets his
body fall in the water. Love was our name, he thinks, but I
couldn't find the name, I couldn't choose it when I should
have. I listened to the noise in vain, I should have tried to
hear what was hidden inside.

The sea opens its embrace for the fisherman who
comes of his own will. This poor man didn't know that
eternal love is fatal. Who will guide him now? Who will

usher him to the kingdom of death now that he is ready to enter? The task belongs to the sea. Who will explain to the fisherman that the fish loved him as long as he seemed strong, but summoned his annihilation when he proved weak—not merely among humans, which is understandable, but also just with himself. Someone must explain. But that task does not belong to the sea. The sea, as wise as it is vast, knows that death is all-powerful because it overcomes suffering.

Below, the rock slowly opens to receive the fisherman who arrives in surrender. Like a mother, the sea will keep its beloved in its womb, and never allow him to be reborn.

1968–1972–1976–77

2.

I bought a candied wafer-wheel and walked to a terrace café
that overlooked the street. The waiter must never have
grown tired of expressing his amazement—fifty times, a
hundred times a day—at the tourists who think they can easily
consume such huge sweets by themselves; with eyes wide open, he
then looked first at the candied wheel, then at me, and then,
serving me my tea, retreated behind his counter.

The man whose face was as beautiful as death had not appeared yet. Just to spite the waiter, I ate the entire candied
wheel, ordered another pot of tea, and finished reading the
newspaper.

Later I realized that his amazement was genuine. He probably thought I was not a tourist because of the way I spoke and
because I read the local newspaper.

I went inside, approached the counter and paid him; just
then, I was surprised to notice the glass wall in the back. Looking
through, you saw the sky and, just below the base of the counter,

*one or two steeples . . . You could pass through a door and step
on to another terrace with a vaulted ceiling.*

*I walked on to this other terrace and instantly felt dizzy be-
cause of the vast expanse that opened before me. My hand,
searching for something to hold, hit the corner of a table. Below
me was an abyss. A long stairway lead to the bottom where a
fountain took up about an eighth of the courtyard. Lines drawn
from the center to the circumference divided the stone courtyard
into wedges. On one side, there was an ancient palace three stories high that looked like a toy castle below me—its tower
reached the level of my waist.*

*Someone near me whose native language wasn't English
said, "Striking, isn't it?"*

*He must have been sitting at the table that I held on to. An
open notebook in front of him, a pencil in his hand. I nodded in
agreement. His face wasn't severe, but neither did it bear even
the trace of a smile.*

*I approached the edge of the terrace cautiously and, after
getting used to the height, began slowly descending the steps that
already, after the recent renovations, looked worn out. I stopped
on the fourth step, turned my head. His eyes above me were
watching. Behind him, I caught a glimpse of a poster tacked on
the wall. Apart from the word, NOTICE, written in large
green letters, nothing else was legible. I thought it wiser to watch
my step. Somehow, I managed to reach the courtyard divided
into wedges. If the hill slope didn't so much resemble an ancient
theater stage worthy of giants, it would have looked like a steep
mountain cliff. I wanted to see the old palace from a distance.
Walking to the building at the other end of the courtyard, I
came across another poster with the same NOTICE on it. In this
narrow, overcrowded corner where one could neither stand nor
walk freely, I assumed the customary indifference of the tourist,
and read the notice from start to finish.*

THE MAN WHO
MISSES HIS RIDE,
NIGHT AFTER NIGHT

What day is it? The sea. Which body of water? Tuesday
Who walks? The Stingray. Who swims? the cat . . .
from "Riddles for the Well-Behaved"

For years, he lived thinking, I will go to Sazandere, I am going any day now. Had someone visited the place and praised it to him, or had he seen Sazandere on a map or come upon a picture somewhere and become curious, he couldn't say. The only thing he knew was that, each time he thought of going to the sea, he began his journey with Sazandere in mind, but whether it was because he felt lazy and agreed to accompany his friends to another beach, or because each time the roads happened to be bad or the buses weren't running, he had never managed to get there.

He'd loved the sea for as long as he could remember. Each time he swam, every time his arms were cutting through the water and he watched the gash that almost opened on the water's surface closing back with relentless defiance, whenever he saw his legs swaying inside this cool, colorful gelatinous expanse, he would experience and grasp life with his whole being. From every beach, he brought home pebbles and shells so that he should never be without the sea. Winter after winter, he stared at the shells, the pebbles, and waited for the days when he would again soak up the sea with every pore of his body. In every fish he ate, he tried to retrieve the smell of the seaweed and the beaches; he lent an ear to the breeze rustling the leaves on tree branches, and to the machines that sound like heartbeats, trying to find in these sounds the waves crashing against the shore, the sea's beating heart.

He'd decided to live in a landlocked city, thinking that he would love the sea all the more and would forever postpone the day from arriving when he—human as he was— might grow tired of what he loved so dearly; it had seemed clever somehow, as if he needed to deceive himself, not realizing the futility of such deceptions. . . . His city was full of giant poplars that lined the streets and yards, row after showy row; with spring's arrival, as they donned their green abundant leaves and sounded their rustling, they became more than trees, they evoked the undulant sea, the gentle swaying of boats. While watching and watching those poplars, he became the sea, he became the boat, and he became the fish; he disproved the old proverb about the fish climbing the poplar.

And long after the poplars were filled with leaves, a bird would come and begin to sing after midnight. For hours, it would repeat its brief song made of two notes, one high, another low, sounded at fixed intervals. Was it the horned owl, called the Bird of Isaac? He could never figure it out. The residents of the city who stayed up late had somehow forgotten all about bird songs. Whom could he ask, how could he find out? Yet while the bird's exact name eluded him, he did know that, once this song arrived, the time had come for him to return to the sea. That's when he would pour salt in the water he drank in his dreams, transforming his limbs into sturgeon, and all the curves of his body into jellyfish, to wander the seaweed forests and plunge into currents of mackerel. Then, one morning, sleep would release him and he would head for the sea.

Everywhere in the city, the poplars had greened themselves anew. The bird had sung its song again. Yet, this year, neither the poplars nor the bird stirred the sea in his heart; this had never happened before. Still, years of habit made him believe he had to go to the sea; he could think of nothing more beautiful than the sea, he could not forget that he was born in the sea, and therefore, he had to go.

He noticed the change in his heart but couldn't explain it. He did not dwell on his feelings much. Since he sensed a change, wouldn't it be best to finally go to Sazandere, the place that had been eluding him for years? And this is what he did; without telling anyone, he left, first arriving in this big coastal city; as soon as he got off the bus, he asked for the terminal where he could pick up the bus to Sazandere, and learned that it was across the street; when he entered through the terminal gate, he found himself swallowed by the deafening rumble, a terrific tempest of noise.

Passing through the terminal gate, he had closed his eyes. Just the way he did when diving off a steep cliff, letting himself into the emptiness. As soon as he opened his eyes, he felt his legs tensing up—ready to start the push-and-spring motion—as if to free himself from the noise by rising to its surface. Yet the noise engulfed him like the water of a muddy lake, wrapped his body with its weeds—like the wild branches of a thousand trees—and assaulted his whole being; it had no surface to which one could escape. He could escape from this lake, this swamp of voices, only if he found the Sazandere bus, only if he sought refuge inside the vehicle, and let the road carry him away.

He thought of the lazy fish that traveled the seven seas by attaching itself to giant, bloodthirsty sharks, moving at the speed of sharks without a flick of its fins . . . Just as he certainly couldn't name the bird that sang on the poplar, neither could he recall the name of this fish. Maybe it started with Rem, Remo, or something like that.

again he saw himself walking through the open bazaar and at the same time

They were pulling him from every direction. The buses were going to Sazlı, Görencik, Madrabaz, to Kuyulu, Arifköy, here, there, leaving right away, hurry, hurry . . .

slowly, slowly he was walking through the silence

On the way to this coastal city, he had started to doze off in the bus and found himself entering a liminal space— half memory half dream—beyond the landlocked city's bazaar surrounded by the poplars. Was this tempest of noise making him more numb than awake?

he stood somewhere outside the open-air bazaar, as if he was filming it, and he watched himself walking slowly from one end of the bazaar to the other

He randomly stopped somewhere in the noise. Hands were grabbing him by his shoulders; little children, bus-drivers' aides, leeched on to his legs. They wanted to take him to all sorts of places—Gerdir, Baltepe, Bodur, Sul-taneşiği, Kuşlar. But before he could say, I want to go to Sazandere, those holding his arms shook him off—as if shaking mud off their sleeves—and flung him toward the farther reaches of the noisy lake. Breathing with difficulty, he struggled to move through the crowd.

he descended the steps to the open-air bazaar. It was a day other than Sunday, a day neither before nor after the bazaar day, neither when the produce was hauled in nor when the after-bazaar trash and dirt were collected, a day in the middle of the week, a desolate bazaar, without the stands, with-out the carts, without the poles and beams, without the umbrellas, from end to end

He was about to test whether or not he had learned

how to free himself from the people leeching on to his arms and legs and pulling him in every direction. He didn't even need to say Sazandere. . . . He was again advancing through the rumble, the heat, the oil smell, toward the depths of the bus terminal.

from end to end, he walked slowly through the silence. From the top of the stairs, as well, from the street, he watched himself. There was a breeze. The kind that brought rain. The dust particles swirling off the ground got caught in the hems of his pants, his sleeves, his ears, his hair. Scaling up and down the vacant produce stands, the sandy platforms surrounded by cinder blocks, he walked slowly through the bazaarless bazaar, from end

In the hottest spot with the most pungent smells of sweat and oil, they pointed to—as if cursing—three vehicles lined up in the remotest corner of the terminal. From afar, he was at least able to see the Sazandere buses; he walked toward them.

from end to end; as much as he was conscious of his walking, he also watched himself from afar and from outside, from the street overlooking the open-air bazaar, he watched himself watching through the eye of his camera. A solitary man passing through the silent and desolate bazaar, being filmed by a man—that is, himself—standing behind the bazaar; as he walked through the bazaar, from end to end

Approaching the spot he'd been shown, he saw one of the three buses leaving; deafened by the noise, his ears registered not even the slightest sound, and the bus glided away as if in a silent movie. He wanted to run after it. All the people crowding the terminal seemed to have moved in front of him, blocking his path.

and as he walked from end to end, suddenly a folk tune that a friend of his used to sing lovingly ar-

rived from his youth and, moving through the
silent desolation, found its way to his consciousness . . . *when the wind rouses its sea, its wavy sea*
. . . Yet the tune had other verses that sang of the
poplars, of Aksaray's shady poplars. The poplars
here surrounded the bazaar on all four sides. Tall,
swaying. And in their midst, in the vast desolation
of the bazaar, there was only the wind—the harbinger of rain; in that vast expanse, from end to
end

He wanted to shout, but he couldn't hear his voice, as
in dreams. By the time he reached the corner, only one
bus remained. Out of breath, he asked the driver who had
suddenly appeared before him when the bus would leave.
"It will not leave," the driver said, "this one's going nowhere . . ." Exasperated, he stood frozen, took a deep
breath, cleared his throat, and then, with the calmest voice
he could muster, he asked, "Just a minute ago, there were
three buses here. Where did the other two go?" The driver's face and voice clearly showed his surprise at the question. "Where else would they go," he said, "one went to
Gündüzlü, the other, to Arifköy . . ."

as he walked, crossing diagonally the desolation of
the bazaar, from end to end, as he stood on the
street, outside the bazaar, and again saw in the
keen gaze of multiple lenses the figure of himself
walking, he knew that the man walking amid the
swirls of dust, in that deadly silence, didn't even recall the sea. But was it the man watching from the
street, or the one walking in the bazaar from end
to end

There would be no buses departing for Sazandere that
night, the dispatcher told him. For a moment, he felt uncertain. He could take another bus, go to a place he knew,
postpone his trip to Sazandere until another summer. As
usual. But he decided against the idea. When he left the

terminal and found himself back on the street, his mind was assaulted by the Mediterranean night noise—grown all the wilder at this late hour—the cacophony of cars, the open-air cinemas, the sherbet and nut vendors, the hordes of people. He felt tired; little by little, his ears began to hear beyond the rumble. He found himself a hotel, went to bed, fell asleep.

Rising from sleep, he was still walking in the bazaar. Fully awake, he began to curse at his stupidity. Between the flashbacks to the bazaar and the confusion of running around, he had forgotten what he should have asked. If all the buses that were supposed to go to Sazandere had gone to other places, then, had *another* bus actually gone to Sazandere? If there was going to be one tonight, where would it leave from? Those giving him directions had misled him either from ignorance or just out of malice. Would the same thing happen tonight? Even if there were a bus leaving during the day, he refused to go to the terminal. In the blistering heat, it would be foolish to sit and bake inside a bus, when he could enjoy the beach nearby. He rode the tram, went to the sea. Around evening, he returned, ate a good meal, and stopped back at the bus terminal to find the dispatcher. According to the dispatcher, three buses could be leaving for Sazandere, each thirty minutes apart: the first one always left; if enough passengers showed up, the second one left; and if there were more passengers, the third one. . . . He asked for the schedule, and after briefly wandering the streets that were slowly coming alive, returned thirty minutes before the first bus's departure time, and began to wait at the specified spot.

Either because he had somewhat grown used to the noise tonight or because his excitement allowed him to turn a deaf ear, he felt as though he weren't inside the terminal but somewhere far away. As if he were again in the bazaar. . . . As if the sea was slowly receding into the distance. Yet here he was, trying to go to the sea, with a

determination he had never shown before; he was waiting
for the bus, as if watching for prey. It was the man in the
bazaar who had forgotten the sea. But was it the man
watching from the street who knew this, or the one walking in the bazaar

> from end to end? The man walking in the bazaar
> thought of death awaiting him at the end of his
> path; rather, the one filming him knew that the
> other thought of this. Why film on the day when
> the bazaar is dead and not on one of the three days
> of the week when it is brimming with life? the man
> on the street was thinking perhaps, standing atop
> the stairs. Yet he wasn't alone in thinking these
> thoughts; they also occurred to the man walking in
> the bazaar. Lifting his head—as if he wished to
> avoid his other self with the camera but in the end
> expected that he would see him—he glanced at the
> poplars. The nocturnal bird had probably already
> arrived to sing among those poplars. Then, avoid-
> ing his other self with the camera, he fixed his gaze
> at his feet moving in front of him, and continued
> walking. He was walking, filming himself walking.
> When he reached the other end of the bazaar

The more he realized that he was mixing three or four
different spans of time together, the more he became
confused. While his bus approached, he felt drowsy—
probably because he was road weary—and he was split in
two, between the man walking in the bazaar and the one
filming him from above. Plunging into the noise of the
terminal did not free him from this liminal space. Walking
in the terminal, he was three people in one, standing both
alongside and separate from the two in the bazaar, as if
watching them. At night, in his dream, he had continued
to experience the endless transience. Even now he was
absorbed in the men in the bazaar. As last night's dream
multiplied threefold inside his memory of the dream, he

now became fourfold, as he watched himself standing in the terminal, and stood outside of everything he saw . . . It would never end. I'm multiplying as in a hall of mirrors, I must be tired, upset, it must be the mishaps piling one on top of the other, he thought, trying to reassure himself.

All of a sudden, he noticed a rickety bus arrive where he had been waiting. It was finally the hour of departure. The bus was falling to pieces, one of those vehicles that had gorged on miles and miles of road over the years and were mockingly called "vintage," as if to denigrate the beauty of genuine vintage buses. When he asked whether it was going to Sazandere, the driver gave a vague response that sounded equally like yes or no. By now accustomed to the hubbub around him, the man was able to hear his own voice and question clearly. The driver was obviously of the ilk who did not rub shoulders with the lower life forms called passengers. He decided to wait a while. Another bus arrived, this one even more rundown than the first. He went to its driver and repeated his question. This time, the response sounded close to a definitive yes. He got in, found a seat that wasn't altogether threadbare and still had some spring to it. He could even stretch his legs if no one sat next to him . . . The bazaar reappeared before his eyes.

> he had reached the other end of the bazaar and was now jumping over the low fence to get to the street. Far away and up on high, the other man— that is, still himself—was packing up his camera and leaving. The filming of the man walking through the desolate bazaar was finished. The reels would be placed in the box

Just as he was emerging from the haze of his dream, a loud clanging nearby startled him. Had he fallen asleep again? The bus that had arrived first was leaving. Before he could gather his bags and lunge out of the bus, that crumbly battered object had already slipped through the crowd and disappeared. He couldn't see the driver of his bus. He found someone standing by and asked where the bus that had just left was going. "I think to Soğukgöl." He breathed a sigh of relief. "When is this bus leaving?" he asked. "Not any time soon, its driver went to bed a while ago, he must already be sleeping . . . This bus leaves in the morning, headed for Kazlar." Like a madman, he ran in every direction, and found the dispatcher. Except for him, everyone seemed to know where the Sazandere buses left from. Not a single person was looking for the bus to Sazandere, except for him. Yet if the place he imagined was also real, people would have to be going there. The berated dispatcher replied, "The bus to Sazandere left quite a while ago; besides it leaves from that corner," pointing to the spot just next to the terminal gate. What would be the point of arguing with him? "You must have misunderstood what I said," the dispatcher added. "Each night, only one bus leaves for Sazandere, and tonight's already left." He felt defeated. But he would return to-morrow night. After all he had endured, he could not think of not going to Sazandere.

He spent the second day again by the sea. In the evening, he went to the terminal, but couldn't find the dis-patcher. He checked every single bus, one by one. He went everywhere he was shown, and everywhere he was shown somewhere else. His bag on his shoulder, his suit-case in his hand, he was tossed about and cast in every di-rection, but he could not find the bus he was supposed to ride. Other buses were going to all kinds of places, some he knew, some he didn't. Yet somehow, few people knew about the Sazandere buses, or rather, those claiming to know provided unreliable information. He was about to collapse with exhaustion. As he walked by the place where he had twice asked about the Sazandere buses, he asked again and was told, "Ten minutes ago, it left from here."

The next night, he missed the bus again. And the night after the next, and the following night. Yet, he was becoming a master of the chase; clearly, the bus would not be able to elude him forever; he would inevitably catch it soon. During the day, he stopped going to the sea. Besides, once he made it to Sazandere, he would never come out of the sea. He sluggishly lay in bed till nighttime, barely ate anything, didn't even read books, felt too lazy even to glance at the evening newspapers he kept buying, and tossed them under the bed instead. Each night he returned to the bus terminal, having overcome the anxiety that he might forget the sea or miss the bus, instead savoring more and more the pleasure of playing a game according to its rules. The bus could not escape him anymore. And that was exactly what happened. On the sixteenth night, he trapped the Sazandere bus, as if trapping an animal in a corner.

Yet the night before, something had happened that undermined all his efforts, and ruined his sense of victory in having found the bus at last. The dispatcher had pulled him behind a vehicle and said, "Brother, you come night after night, I know. I feel like I should tell you. Actually, eight of the buses that go somewhere else may stop in Sazandere, and they do stop there, either on the way to their destination or afterwards. But because it's remote, the drivers would rather not go there, unless they have to. They charge more money, they fight with the passenger, and try to get him off the bus in the middle of the road. That's why the residents of the place travel together, always riding in the same bus, and once on the road, the driver stops being crotchety. But when you're a lone passenger, no driver would tell you that he's going there, so you should know. Now, if by some coincidence, there are other passengers . . . then, yes, maybe, you get to go. Besides, what about all the other countless locations you can travel to, did the plague pass through them?" These words robbed him of the joy he would have been feeling right now, but what could he do?

Tonight, when he found the bus as if it had been placed there with his own hands, he was told that all the passengers had arrived and the bus was leaving right away. He got in. It was a brand new sparkling motor coach. All the passengers were in their seats, some curled asleep, others getting ready to sleep. As soon as he took his seat, the engine started to run, and they traveled with the carefree weightlessness of a ship, leaving the noise behind. In less than ten minutes, they were gliding on the highway, faster and faster, through darkness so complete that they could see not even a fleck of light. So it is possible, he prided himself, when one works hard, better yet, when one desires something enough, if one knows how to desire. Just then, he came to himself, as if someone slapped him. In light of the dispatcher's words the night before, his pride was laughable and little else . . .

The interior lights had long since been turned off. He could hear the snores all around him. He could fall asleep, too, so that he wouldn't arrive tired in Sazandere.

Later he was awakened. It was still dark. The bus had stopped. He tried to listen, while still feeling drowsy. He couldn't hear the sound of the sea. "What's the matter?" he asked the young man who woke him up. He was the driver's assistant who, like all his peers, checked the engine throughout the trip, repaired it if needed, offered the passengers cologne and distributed bottles and bottles of cold water; his face was swollen because his youthful sleep was constantly interrupted, and he knew to behave politely even though his polite shirt could barely restrain his brusque, unrefined youthfulness. "We've arrived; this is where you get off," he said. Cheerfully confident that people ought to know their jobs, the man decided not to argue and descended from the bus. In the darkness, someone handed him his suitcase. Besides, he was the only passenger left in the bus; everyone else had already gotten off at earlier stops. Before he could even feel the ground under his feet, he noticed the bus speeding away, with all the power of its newness, leaving an intense dust smell behind. He was obviously all alone in the darkness. He waited. The dust stopped burning his throat. He listened. There was no sound of the sea. He lifted his nose; there was no salt smell either. He was surprised that he wasn't angry. He was surprised that he wasn't surprised. He adjusted the shoulder strap of his bag, took a step or two, and felt as if his feet were sinking in the sand. No, not as if, they were literally sinking in the sand. He put his suitcase on the ground, and he bent down; this wasn't the familiar sand of the beach or the sea. Flour-like, very fine-grained, it was like no sand he knew. In the seamless silence, the bazaar flashed through his mind and faded just as swiftly. He wasn't wondering whether or not he was in Sazandere. In the pure silence, the sea would have made itself heard, even if it were far away. There was no sound, no sea breeze; this didn't sadden him either. If nothing else, he was sure that he had not taken the wrong bus. Besides, no sooner had he settled in his seat than he had repeatedly instructed the driver's assistant where he was supposed to get off. He walked a few more steps, sinking as he walked. He no longer cared about the sea. Nor about Sazandere. He only experienced wonder. True, he was a traveler, anything could have gone wrong, he ought to have been prepared; still, like all passengers, deep down he had hoped that all would be well, that fortune would smile on him; this was a secret, elusive hope. Was he standing on a seabed where the water had receded over the years? He began to walk in no particular direction, abandoning his suitcase. There was no point in carrying a load or in thinking, for that matter. Now he was climbing a small hill, he could tell. A sand dune. He tossed away his bag also. Was Sazandere—or wherever he happened to be—

actually a desert? He laughed. Yet, little by little, a wave of anxiety spread from his heart to his stomach, and then to his arms. He walked a little further.

All of a sudden, at the bottom of a dune, he saw a row of windows, glowing with lights. He walked down and, turning the corner of the wall with the windows, he came upon a door, outlined by a set of turquoise glass panes through which intense light was flowing. He made a fist, and he knocked on the center of the door with his middle knuckles. Before he could pull away his hand, the door opened.

A very old man stood in front of him. Smiling as if he knew the visitor, he said, "Welcome," with a shaky voice, "welcome, we were beginning to worry. Come in, here, have a seat by the stove . . ."

"You must be confusing me with someone you've been waiting for," the man attempted to say, but didn't; he noticed all of a sudden that he was terribly cold. He entered and gladly walked toward the stove facing the door. "So very long your place has been waiting for you," said the brittle faltering voice that followed him, "so very long we've been waiting for you, thinking, he'll join us this year, or next year . . ."

The man sat in the empty space evidently reserved for him in front of the stove, stretched his hands and feet toward the incandescent flames. He looked to his right, then to his left. On both sides were ancient faces, faces scored with wrinkles, snow-haired heads that drooped toward hollow chests; they were smiling senselessly at him with their drawn cheeks, their toothless mouths; their eyes, sunk in their sockets, staring absently at his eyes.

1968–1972

3.

*T*he tour of the ancient palace must have lasted two hours. Shortly after I entered the museum, I found him standing in front of a fifteenth-century painting. He turned, looked at me with what seemed like the beginning of a smile forming in the corner of his mouth. With his chin, he pointed at the painting and moved to another gallery. I sat in front of the painting. It was the work of an ordinary "small master," clearly aware of the conventions of his period, but neither faithfully following them nor really subverting them. It depicted an event in the courtyard of the ancient palace. Since the palace was drawn with utmost concern for verisimilitude, the activities in the courtyard also must have been depicted realistically. Yet, the courtyard was not divided into wedges in the painting; rather, it resembled a large chessboard, a round chessboard. . . . A large crowd was gathered on one side. On the squares stood men in strange costumes of a different style from the clothes worn by the spectators. As far as I could tell, the *costumes did not belong to any specific era. The green or purple bands loosely tied around the waist differentiated the multicolored gowns. Obviously, two teams were involved in a game. A medieval game. The strangeness of the costumes brought to mind not the Renaissance but the mysterious symbolism of the Middle Ages. At least to the mind of a stranger like me who had learned the history merely from books. The identical expression on the players' faces made one think it was a game not for pure entertainment but carefully played (who knows, perhaps even anxiously).*

A game played anxiously, it must be, I said to myself. Let's see what else I would come up with. . . .

The more I looked at the painting, the more I realized that the players on the purple team were more anxious, tense and reserved than those on the green team. The greens appeared wilder, more agile and stern. Leaves, thorns and roots hung on their costumes, as though the men had crossed through a dense forest to arrive here. On the chains around their necks were animal figurines — horses, wolves, leopards.

The painting grew larger before my eyes. I could better discern its details.

His voice startled me; I suddenly realized how close I was standing to the painting.

"How it lures the observer, don't you agree?" he said. "No wonder the nomads love the water." I saw him smile for the first time. To look at him was intoxicating. "I'll return," he said afterwards, "I imagine you'd like to hear about the game in this painting."

He disappeared again; as if a door had opened before him, even though he was standing in front of a solid wall.

A sentence from a foreign novel came to mind. "Between your hands . . . Even when they are in your hands. . . . Even when they are inside your palm . . ." I couldn't pin it down. How to say it in Turkish? ". . . inside your palm are creatures of escape."

I could leave the translation for later. I was beginning to feel hungry. I could think of the Turkish version of the sentence while eating. First I had to tour the museum.

Two hours later, he reappeared at the end of a long corridor, pointing with his hand to a gallery of sculptures that I'd visited when first entering the museum; then he left.

I walked quickly and entered the room. What did he want to show me? Was I supposed to notice a particular object among busts no different from all the ones I'd grown tired of seeing in one museum after another? Beside a couple of deities with broken arms and wings, there was also a thirteenth-century gravestone. The likeness of the dead was carved on it. Just then I understood what he wanted me to see. On the gravestone, among the folds of the elegant gown, a horse figurine hung at the end of a chain delicately carved around the man's neck. The small motif under his chipped-off feet resembled a poppy or a blackberry branch. The stone.

• • •

It grew dark while I was eating my dinner. I decided to climb the stairs and drink my coffee at the place where I first saw him. He was sitting at the same table. Here, it was still light while down below it had turned completely dark. Although the shop windows were illuminated, the street lamps were not lit yet. I said nothing and sat across him.

"Will you take part in the game?" he asked.

A MEDIEVAL MONK

To Adalet Cimcoz
(I read this piece to him in Istanbul.
It was the end of December.
He didn't get to see it published.)

I n the beginning, the middle, and the end of everything is the image of a man with his animal around
his waist. Everything gathers around this image:
everything accumulates, falls into place, comes to life, and
unwinds.

This is the image of a medieval *abdal*. A wandering
monk shrouded in a robe, his eyes hidden underneath the
tired, worn-out hat that has long lost its original softness
and assumed the shape of his head, his bare feet covered
with large bruises—a medieval monk. In the bitter cold,
his body has shrunk and shrunk until nothing is left of him
other than a hump and a sash. He must have decided
against sleeping outside in the darkness that would follow
the daylight now thrusting into his eyes like branding
irons, so he is walking toward the caravanserai that looks
like crouched camels on the distant hillside. If he can just
get there, even at dusk, if he can find a little place to curl
up beside the walls, it would be enough.

At sunset, this monk will not have reached the gate of

the caravanserai. Dust-swirls stirred by his tired dragging feet now rise up to his waist. He is the only traveler on this road. The road clouds up in dust only around him. Now and then he starts, as if seized by spasms, by shivers. But he alone knows that these spasms, these shivers have nothing to do either with the steppe wind arriving at nightfall or with the convulsion of his stomach that hasn't received even a morsel of bread since morning. No one but the monk knows the claws, the teeth that rip through his robe and scrape and pierce his flesh, no one but he knows this pain of ripping and piercing, because no one has yet seen the half jerboa-half mongoose, this pinkish-furred animal with flesh-eating incisors and claws, that he has been carrying inside the folds of his sash. Once in his youth, he had spent the night inside a mountain cave and the animal had crawled inside his sash and settled there; ever since, he has been carrying it with him year after year. Try as he would, beating has not dissuaded the animal; he couldn't run away from it, nor could he bring himself to kill it. It's not true that he has shared his every morsel with the animal; at the most they have shared every third morsel. And the animal has hurt him only in times of intense hunger, just like now. The monk has grown so accustomed to living with the animal that he has even stopped marveling at its resilience.

Besides shelter, he must also find a morsel to eat tonight. He has been walking on this steppe for days; there isn't even a crumb left in his bag.

As for those staying at the caravanserai tonight, they belong to another time. A wandering mob, carefree and noisy, they are men who have arrived on small, swift-as-the-wind metal-plated steeds at this forsaken way station on the steppe which has known no mounts other than camels. The animals take up the courtyard, and the travelers have claimed all the sleeping quarters that the caravanserai can offer. They must be tired because they have eaten all the provisions in their bags and lain down to sleep without even removing their dusty boots.

By the time the monk arrives, the gates will have been closed and darkness fallen long since. In the time of the monk, the gates are not reopened before dawn. As for those already inside, they belong to a time when they no longer remember why the gates cannot be opened—if not to let people in, at the least to let people out.

The monk stands before the gate, yet still outside. In the wind. Before darkness settles, this is the last thing he sees: the caravanserai that had appeared leaning against the hill—he had stared and stared at it since this morning—actually stands quite far ahead of the hill. Exposed on all four sides, it offers no refuge. Because it's not a light breeze we are talking about, but a harsh bitter wind, the kind that squashes you to the ground, forces you to recoil and shrink . . . Pacing before the unyielding gates does not help either. The animal's claws pierce into his flesh deeper and deeper. They almost dig into his bowels. He must feed its hungry belly, otherwise, whether he beats it, kicks it, or tries to grab it by its neck to hurl it away, nothing will change; these are schemes he has tried for years and long given up trying.

He curls up his body and squats inside one of the recesses on the richly carved stones rising alongside the gate.

The men inside the caravanserai lie asleep on wooden benches that look more like tables than beds. There is nothing beneath the outstretched bodies; over them are the covers pulled and dragged from the metal-plated steeds, some look like blankets, others don't. One bed is empty, but at its foot is a crumpled blanket. Sleep must not have visited the man lying on it. He is awake, wandering in the dark.

This man first wanders among the beds, then, walking into the courtyard, he looks at the watchman. He still appears young, his hair and beard yet untouched by gray, his shoulders unsunk, his backbone unbent. Yet given that he cannot sleep, he must have left his youth behind him.

He is the one who sees the monk, the solitary figure walking up the dusty road in the evening's crimson hour. He is the one who tells the innkeeper that he has just seen someone coming up the road, who asks him to delay closing the gates a little longer. But the innkeeper lives in the time of the monk. He has been ordered to close the gates before the sun sets below the horizon. Nothing can be done.

The man is searching for a way to let in the monk who must have reached the gates by now. This is why he looks at the watchman.

To let the monk in, he must find the gap in the wall that will open years from now, hundreds of years from now. Yet for the time being, the only crack is in the inside corner of one of the arched piers supporting the innkeeper's tower in the middle of the courtyard.

He keeps walking. Passing underneath the arches, walking alongside the walls in order to elude the watchman. And in the end, he finds what he has been looking for.

He finds it by walking and walking alongside the walls solid as a fortress. In the corner where the sidewall of the courtyard meets the actual frame of the caravanserai, the ground is inexplicably hollowed a little, the bottommost stone of the wall appears slightly out of place. But opening a hole here would require centuries. Yet, ever since arriving with his friends in the caravanserai that stands in the middle of this endless plateau, the man has become helplessly caught in the time of the caravanserai, in the time of the monk who is waiting outside—and who must be shivering, like him, in the wind.

Yet . . . All of a sudden . . . The man will be astonished by the sight of a hole wide enough for a man opening through the wall, and someone in a monk's garb slipping into the courtyard, whispering some words in a voice muffled by layers and layers of dust.

Understanding the whispers takes a difficult process of deciphering, like reading hieroglyphs. As the monk silently moves toward the sleeping quarters, the man wants to run after him and catch up; in the meantime, he is able to figure out the monk's words: "I thought the walls were solid and walked and walked till I came upon the freshly dug opening. It wasn't there when I passed by the first time around. As if it opened afterwards." And for this reason, the monk now offers praises to god.

Catching up with the monk, the man finds him searching around. He must be hungry, the man thinks and, reaching for his sack at the head of his bed, he takes out buns filled with cheese and meat, wrapped in plastic wrap, and hands them to him. . . .

The monk brings the bun not to his mouth but to his sash. Between the dusty folds of fabric, a muzzle emerges, and two claws. The rest of the animal remains hidden. But little by little the bread disappears into the claws and the muzzle. . . .

The man stares at the monk in utter astonishment, while the monk fixes his eyes on the animal and watches silently. Evidently satisfied, the animal disappears among the folds of the sash. A small morsel of bread falls to the ground. The monk then picks up that morsel, blows it clean and puts it in his mouth. The man hands the monk another bun. The monk quietly takes it, sits on the bench by the wall, and begins to eat, chewing it slowly, very slowly. There must not be a single tooth left in his mouth.

The sounds of snoring swell and die, wave after wave. The winds, the monk wonders, do they also blow like this around here. The man stares at him.

Then, finding the moonlight insufficient, the man walks under the arch and enters the sleeping quarters;

going to his bed he takes a lantern out of his sack and returns, walking with sure steps, the lantern illuminating his path.

In the yellow artificial glow, he begins to draw the picture of the monk chewing his bread. He draws with his hands, his fingers. He draws in the air. Draws the picture of the monk who is caught in his gaze. The picture takes shape little by little; the monk who stands within the drawn lines becomes two-dimensional little by little.

He must have decided that his drawing is finished; he lowers the lantern to the ground, and as though casting the two-dimensional monk in a frame, he holds him and lays him on the ground. Aided by the slanted light, he briefly scans to find the right spot to place his signature; he then pulls from his pocket a long skewer-like object that resembles a carver's knife. Pressing it against the monk's bare flank, he begins to sign. Just then, something unexpected happens: even before the signature is finished, the monk open his toothless mouth and—without raising himself up or even moving in the slightest—starts emitting ear-splitting noises and coughs. The man pulls his pen away. The monk does not stop. The coughing turns to vomiting. First, out comes the bread he'd just finished chewing; then he spits blood, dark clots of blood, then his lungs, piece after piece, dark and bloody.

Terrified, the man runs away from the monk. He doesn't forget to pick up his lantern. He throws himself in his bed and even pulls his blanket over his face. When his terror subsides somewhat, he is able to listen for sounds. The coughing has stopped. The retching becomes less frequent. Soon it, too, dies out. After a time, he thinks he hears footsteps approaching from the outside. A childhood fear inside him raises its head from the place where it has been hiding for years. "What if the innkeeper comes, sees my signature and blames me . . ." The men, more precisely, the steps, recede. It must have been the night watchman. Quiet returns to him. Outside, too, is calm. Everything that happened defies reason. He almost believes that he has been dreaming.

Yet . . . All of a sudden . . . He feels a sharp piercing sensation on his leg, inching up. Without seeing, without looking, he knows. He attempts to strangle the animal with all his strength, while screaming as loudly as his throat can muster. Those awakened run to him. The innkeeper rushes in with the night watchman. After much struggle, they wrench the animal from his thigh and, rushing to the courtyard, they pass under the arch. The man follows them, blood oozing through his torn clothes. In the glow of the lanterns, he scans the stone-tiled rooms, the ground, all around, but he can see nothing. The men had tied a rope around the animal's neck in order to wrench it from his thigh. Now the animal dangles at the end of the rope. At the end of the courtyard, the man holding the rope whirls the animal over his head a few times then slings it off, as if slinging a stone. With the rope tied around its neck, the animal flies over the walls and disappears from sight. Then the innkeeper sends everyone back to bed.

The next morning when his friends leave to take to the road, the man stays behind. No matter how much they plead, they can't convince him. The man tells them that he will never again set foot outside the caravanserai gate. His friends plan to roam the region before returning to a city located not too far from the caravanserai. They decide to meet five days later in that city.

The man stays in the caravanserai for four days and four nights. In the morning of the fifth day, he gets on his metal-plated steed and, bidding farewell to everyone, leaves through the gate. He thinks he can reach the city where he will find his friends about noon.

Just outside the gate, as he turns the corner for the main road, something leaps from behind a rock and, in a flash, falls onto his lap. The man doesn't even get a chance to scream. This time the animal nestles inside his pocket without hurting him the least bit, and they get on the main road. Anxious about the claws that could pierce through his pocket and rip into his belly, his hip, the man reaches the city shortly before noon. But nothing happens. Inside the pocket of his light summer coat, there is a bulge as small as that of a crumpled handkerchief, so small that, when the man reunites with his friends, no one notices the animal in his pocket. The man is determined: He will do what the monk couldn't do. The first time he feels the claws in his flesh, he will stick his hand into his pocket, pull the animal out, and before the eyes of his friends— who, on that night he'd screamed, had mocked and derided him because he'd cost them their sleep, and who had seen his refusal to leave the caravanserai the next morning as a sign of his agitated mind—yes, before their eyes, he will strangle the animal. If it fights death, he will cut its throat with the first sharp object he can find, or shatter its skull with a rock.

He waits. The animal does not move. But every time he brushes his hand over his pocket—secretly, letting no one notice—the man can feel the animal's warmth, its breathing.

He waits. Yet, near evening, it suddenly occurs to him: to get rid of the animal, to strangle it, to slit its throat or shatter its skull, he doesn't have to wait until it claws him. It's madness to act as if he's considering carrying the animal in his pocket for the rest of his life. Why the monk had carried the animal, or for how long, the man doesn't know but, all along, he has supposed that it was for an entire lifetime—and he's now behaving as if he believes that.

At dinner, a large knife lies before them. He slips his hand inside his pocket, and facing no resistance, pulls the animal out. He lays it on the table; and just when he raises the knife to slit its throat, his friends start shouting and screaming. They grab his arms and hands. Tell him he should be locked up. Has he gone mad? Why kill the poor animal when he should instead tend to its needs, given that he's been carrying it around in his pocket?

Lifting him up by his elbows, they carry the man away from the table and lay him in bed.

At night, when everyone has retreated, the animal that escaped during the commotion comes back, finds its way into the man's bed, rips open his belly with its claws, and chews his bowels, and tears them into shreds. In the morning, his friends find the man's dead body covered in cooled, congealed blood. They could trace the animals bloody prints to the middle landing of the stairway. From there on, the blood on its claws must have dried.

They bury their friend; dispirited by the experience, they decide to return to their own city, and mount their metal-plated steeds. A few hours later, they see a man walking in the middle of the road, robed like a medieval monk; they see him only out of the corners of their eyes, as they flash past him and hurry on. The monk has been walking fast and, noticing the dust cloud rolling toward him, he barely throws himself to the side of the road in time. He stares at those creatures riding past at lightning speed. He shakes his head for a long time, rubs his eyes, but, looking again, he can no longer see anything on the road—only in the distance, a dust cloud uncoils slowly, slowly. He has no time to waste. Or else he will not be able to reach the caravanserai before the gates close. He continues to walk quickly. Then he slips his hand inside the folds of his sash. The animal's warm, furry back once again feels like the most positive evidence of reality.

1969

4.

*F*irst *I looked at his hands.*

His English sounded north European. He could be German, Dutch or Scandinavian. Or perhaps Austrian, but that didn't occur to me. His accent evoked snow, lakes, pines, elk with tangled antlers. He spoke little, but perhaps because of his accent, I started noticing that the color of his hair was lighter than the dark chestnut shade I'd remembered from the night before; if someone asked me now, I'd say he was blond.

Yet he had the hands of a Mediterranean.

Dark skin paler between the fingers, hands lined with olive-green veins. . . .

The beauty of his hands left an indelible impression in my mind. The darkness rising like water from below covered us up to our knees, but his face was still in the light. He looked swarthy, definitely so, befitting the dark skin of his hands.

Yet, soon, in the last rays of the sun, I would note—

trembling with excitement—that I wasn't mistaken about the golden hue of his hair.

• • •

"If we accept the conventional explanation, the town's ruling family established the game and played it once every decade, to commemorate a ninth-century incident with a rival fiefdom to the north."

Some tourists are over-educated. Before visiting a place, they consult every imaginable source, acquire every bit of information they can find about the place. Although visiting for the first time, they seem to have lived there not for years but for centuries. They know everything from street names to restaurants, from paintings and sculptures in the museums to the history and architecture of the ancient palaces. They have learned more facts than even the residents will ever know about their own town.

He is one of them, I thought to myself. He was now sitting in the dark, his back turned to the lights of the café. The terrace had no lamps so that the people sitting at the tables could better see the courtyard below.

". . . yet, if you ask me, this explanation is fabricated to cover a much older regional celebration. From what I could gather—and given that I have researched all the available sources on the topic, no one is likely to know more—the game was first played during a twelfth-century celebration. At first, it was enacted once every fifty years, but, probably in the fifteenth century, the town decided to hold a game once every ten years. Before that, it's certainly not clear how often it was played. However, whenever the rulers wished to flaunt their wealth, they called for this quite extravagant game . . .

". . . extravagant because the ruler whose team was defeated would pay in gold the ransom necessary for the release of his players. Indeed, in the earliest form of the game, the ransom was paid to save the players from being executed. It seems the winners had the right to execute the losers. . . .

"In short, because of its confrontational origin, the game has always been perceived as a display of power."

He was obviously into history. He neither let me ask many questions nor answered the ones I was able to ask. I gave up wondering where he was from. I stopped asking questions altogether. He was not done with his account; I knew the history of the game, but he had yet to explain its "confrontational origin," "the ninth-century incident," and, especially, the meaning of the costumes.

"What do you say we go out to eat?'

I had just finished eating. "Yes, let's." How well he know that I wouldn't turn him down.

• • •

Yesterday, I had written a sentence on a sheet I subsequently crumpled and discarded. But it stayed with me. I had used the word, "Departed," and thought of its fatal connotation in particular. I swear I had. And yet, in less than twenty-four hours, I was struck, shaken by the realization that the name of the game announced in the NOTICEs around town could be translated as "The Game of Departure."

We were at dinner. He hadn't spoken since we sat face to face. Neither did I say a word. I was angry at my naïveté, thinking that he was relishing my stupidity. But what could I say to him?

Toward the end of the meal, just to calm my growing frustration somewhat, I attempted to say mockingly, "How knowledgeable you are." He frowned but said nothing.

I asked for my bill. I would not speak to him any more, not even greet him.

"I already asked you at the café. Will you take part in the game?"

Somehow I found the strength to leave him by saying, "I don't know."

IN PRAISE OF
THE FEARLESS PORCUPINE

To Ceren, and also to François Filliatre,
now a grown-up man in Paris

"Some time ago, while walking down the street, I saw a man.
Sitting on the edge of the sidewalk, he was filing the quills of a
porcupine. And the porcupine was a fool of fools. As if enjoying a
manicure, the animal had its eyes closed . . ."
—*Feyyaz Karacan,*
from a personal correspondence

Fayyaz's fool-of-fools porcupine is a pretty frequent sight, if you ask me. I don't know whether this porcupine he speaks of had been strolling along the sidewalk. The man might have caught it somewhere else, for instance, in one of the parks. He might have caught the animal at Green Park, then taken the sidewalk across the street in Piccadilly, walked up toward, say, the Royal Academy, and stopping around there, he might have sat down on the curb and attended to his business. And why not! I'm picturing the man with the porcupine on his lap, as he pulls out a nail file from his pocket—cars whizzing by, Englishmen scandalized at the sight of such a spectacle—and my friend, Feyyaz, thinking, I must write about this to Bilge, tittering, ironic . . .

Of course, one can also find porcupines that are not foolish. Yet, once a porcupine is caught and trapped between two knees and realizes that there is nothing it can do, it may well close its eyes and wait for the man's madness to pass, and while waiting, it may open its eyes every now and then, to check whether the man is about to desist, and then it might again close its eyes out of pain, as well as shame.

My porcupine was not a Londoner; it lived in Ankara. I don't think it was foolish, this porcupine from Ankara; on the contrary, I'd like to think that it was the daring kind, venturesome, brave. My praise is for its reckless courage . . .

Brave because, a porcupine though it was, it had taken to dwelling in the city, and recklessly courageous because, one night, it dared to leave its dwelling and discover the world . . .

According to the calendar, spring had arrived. But the weather was still cold. The night fogs were still suffocating. Coal smoke streamed from chimneys on to the street, climbing the soot-filled streets toward Çankaya, like the vapors rising off stagnant ponds. I was walking to my house, covering my nose and mouth as much as I could with my hand and scarf, hurrying through this nauseating, throat-burning smoke that would, in ten or fifteen years, no doubt add a refreshing variety to our lives by bringing upon us sundry new forms of death, each more bizarre than the other.

All of a sudden, something scurried from a yard (more like half a yard and half a plot of dirt) onto the sidewalk. I couldn't figure out what it was. I stopped. It stopped. It wasn't a cat or a rat. I didn't want to frighten it. If it tried to escape, darting on to the street, it would be run over by one of the cars speeding through at that vacant hour. I approached it slowly, cautiously. As I got nearer, the thing looked like it was growing, swelling. I leaned slightly toward it, it didn't move. I leaned further. The light was dim, I had difficulty making out the form. In the end, I recognized:

It was a porcupine. Wherever it may have come from, whatever place it may have abandoned.

I stood next to it, no longer moving. After a while, the swelling subsided somewhat, and the animal extended its nose; then, it hurried toward the street, but soon stopped by the lamppost, on the edge of the sidewalk. I started retreating little by little. If I walked toward it, it would probably throw itself under the cars. It's best to stand back, I said to myself. In any case, the sight of the first car would frighten the animal, and it would probably run back to the yard, who knows, perhaps return to its nest, I thought.

A porcupine in Ankara, strolling down the boulevard, a porcupine out on the street, enjoying a nocturnal promenade, I giggled. It wasn't very small either; it couldn't have been young or inexperienced. It had to be a mature, seasoned porcupine. Who knows, perhaps one that had come out in search of food for its young, and had lost its way . . . Stranger to Ankara, an outsider that hoped to find food on the pavement, on a boulevard . . . Or a porcupine that resembled the one in the comic strip that my friend Jan once described, a porcupine in love with a cactus. Perhaps it had come to Ankara on some legal business but, quickly overcome with longing for that cactus, had fallen to roaming the streets . . .

Truly, what business did it have, this displaced porcupine, on an Ankara boulevard like this? And in the middle of the night?

I thought of the bear cub in the lovely fairy tale written by Anne Frank. The cub trying to find its way in the forest made of legs, feet and shoes, when it ran away from home because it was bored, because it wanted to see the world, even though it knew full well that its mother would be inconsolable. I had read that fairy tale in the pale afternoon light of my room in Rome, surrounded by the strange quiet, and hearing—besides the shrill sound of water running day and night from the fountain on the edge of the bright atrium—the intermittent snores of an Italian enjoying his afternoon nap. I had envisioned the little bear wandering along the main street two hundred meters away from my room. And this porcupine that strolled down an Ankara boulevard, did it also need a fairy tale to make it seem less odd?

But I couldn't imagine anything like, "The porcupine had siblings that demanded all of their mother's attention, and that's why the porcupine got angry and left home." I had no siblings of my own.

Neither could I say, "The porcupine ran away to escape its father's spankings." It was too large to receive any spanking from its father.

I would never know or understand. I returned home, took off my clothes and went to bed. Then I decided to imagine myself as the porcupine, and began to describe:

> Mother was a very wise porcupine. "Don't run, don't go too far," she used to shout after me, like any loving mother would. But she used to add right away, "First grow up; then you can wander off and see the world to your heart's content." That's how I grew up. Constantly awaiting the day when I would travel to all the places worth seeing and knowing in the world, travel without fear, without apprehension. I grew up, yes, but before I could find the time to travel, I had already fathered children, so we moved three lots down and built a nest. And the relocation to the new home was not altogether free of hardship. We had to cross exactly three paved and two dirt roads; we had to carry, feed and protect the young ones; we had to defend ourselves against the dogs and rats that kept accosting us; and we had to set up for ourselves a nest in a suitable corner of this new lot much praised by the neighbors. In the noise and toil of relocating, we had to overcome every dif-

ficulty right away. My eyes saw nothing of the world. After all that we went through, who would call it traveling . . .

The children grew up, new ones arrived, they grew up, too, and new ones followed. I realized I would not be able to cope. Now with greater frequency, itinerant porcupines brought me news from my mother whose eyes could no longer see. So a while ago, I left to visit my mother. I did find my parent's nest, but the old vacant plot was now converted into the tiny yard of a giant mansion. They still lived in their old nest, but lamented bitterly: "We can't even stick our noses out of the nest because of the dogs and cats overrunning the yard." I told them that our plot was still safe somehow. They envied my good fortune and offered thankful prayers to their late neighbor who had recommended the plot to us. Tears streamed from my mother's exhausted eyes while she described their neighbor's death. "It would pain me less if they ate him," she said, "they always want to eat us porcupines; they kill us, rip us to pieces. We are used to it. But they didn't eat him. Why did they have to kill him? And with pickaxes! They ripped and tore him to pieces and tossed him in the soil they had been digging. Then all that soil was hauled away from here . . ."

True, for a moment, they did consider packing up and coming with me to escape the terror and enjoy at least their remaining days among their grandchildren. But my mother said, "This blind and broken body can go nowhere any more; I'd be a burden to you on the road," and she changed her mind. Nor could I stay with them for more than three days. I had to return home. I began to worry.

Fear entered my heart. What if the humans decided to build a house on our plot as well? I took to
the road. I walked . . .

Then I pulled myself together and fell asleep.

The next day I remembered the porcupine and wondered whether it might have been hit and run over. But
who knows, perhaps it had been able to reach home safely.
My timing was off in the story I invented last night . . .
For some reason, it seemed right to imagine that its nest
was located in the half-yard/half-plot of dirt that it had
emerged from. If that was the case, then the porcupine
could not have been returning home. Rather, it was at the
start of its journey, on the way to visit its old mother who
was going blind. But consider a porcupine that spends its
entire childhood and adolescence yearning to travel and
see the world. Would this porcupine now describe a short
jaunt of three blocks as a journey? In fact, this particular
detail was already bothering me and that's why I couldn't
imagine the porcupine would consider the relocation as a
journey, and then this same trip back to visit family would
not be much of a journey either. I still wasn't convinced—
that the animal would be searching for things outside the
particular goal of its journey . . . I was talking nonsense.
Most likely, I would not see the porcupine again. And its
story would thus remain unfinished. Its little stroll down
the street would be a half-believable half-beguiling tale at
the most. I saw a porcupine on a nocturnal stroll along an
Ankara boulevard—this was my only gain, I thought to
myself and decided to be satisfied with the experience.

But as fate would have it, we were to meet again.

Four nights later, we were sitting in the house. The
weather had gotten warmer. The door leading to the yard
was left ajar. The cigarette smoke coming out of the house
was dense enough to forestall the coal smoke getting in.
There were seven or eight of us. We were discussing
books, writing. All of a sudden, I noticed our Italian

neighbors standing by the street lamp and inspecting something. They were bending down, looking, standing back, talking among themselves, then bending again, looking again.

I became worried. My cat was outside. Had something happened to him? I went out to the yard. The old and the young women were standing away a little, looking, while the young woman's husband was doing something with a stick. I couldn't see the tip of the stick and whatever he was doing with it because of the wall. I waited. "That's it," the young woman said. The older one nodded. The man stood up and rested his hand on his hip, as if he had accomplished something important. They were still staring down. Then, all three of them started. Something had jumped on top of the wall. It stayed there. Now I was looking at it also. It was a porcupine. It had to be the one I had seen a few nights ago. Never in history have there been two different porcupines spotted in the same neighborhood in a matter of four nights, I am certain. The rest of my story depends on this very certainty. The young woman told the older one, "Mother, hand us your shawl. We have nothing else to wrap it up with." The man kept poking at the porcupine with his stick, preventing it from swelling or escaping. Then, after much effort and poking, he managed to turn the animal on its back. In this position, they would be able to kill the porcupine easily. Obviously, that's what they had been trying to do all along. Who gave them the right to kill! I shouted: "Leave it alone! *Per favore*, leave the animal alone!" My voice must have sounded strange. The women looked at me; the man, now hesitating, touched the animal with his stick one more time. The young woman said, "Fine, fine, leave it alone, Renzo," then she took the older woman by the arm, and staring in my direction, the two began walking. The man followed them. His steps were unwilling. "What a pity," he said, "it would have made a delicious soup!" I was shocked. Porcupine soup had not occurred to me. I shouted some obscenity in Italian. They didn't hear me. I was glad. A porcupine fallen on the city streets wasn't worth heaping curses on people. How could they have know that I had befriended this porcupine?

Lying on its back, on top of the wall, the animal floundered at first, as soon as it sensed that danger had passed. Next, as if changing its mind, it stopped, and then somehow managed to tumble itself down the wall. It must have fallen on its feet since it flashed past the lamppost and ran across the street to the sidewalk, disappearing from sight.

We briefly talked about the porcupine. I explained that I had seen it the other night. Then we moved on to other topics.

This was a porcupine worth writing about. I felt like I could write about it. Obviously, it was traveling the world, experiencing countless mishaps. It deserved a eulogy, a *procupineade*.

I don't know if it was because I realized that the porcupine's journey could end in the soup-pot, but I didn't want to put myself in its place that night. The *procupineade* couldn't be written like that, I said to myself, and without fretting over the double meaning of my conclusion, I fell asleep.

A few days later, I described the porcupine in a letter to François. A Parisian adolescent, after all, he had not yet traveled to Africa either. Not that I would know whether there are porcupines in Africa or if they take nightly strolls there as well, but I had neither seen nor heard of any porcupine pacing up and down a Parisian boulevard. "Why don't you write about it!" came the reply.

Writing would be fun and good, true, but what did the porcupine think of the world? What stories did it tell, provided that it returned home safely? These I had to imagine.

I thought and decided. The porcupine must have spoken thus:

> Once on the road, I couldn't resist. When would I have found another opportunity like this? As a matter of fact—I later realized—this was the only way to enjoy traveling. On the one hand, you bear the sorrow of those you have left behind, and, on the other hand, you fight the heart-wrenching feeling that there are porcupines to whom you must return. And beyond everything: the road, the vastness, the world . . . You don't squander your time, you try to make every moment count, returning home in the same way—albeit by way of long roundabout detours. Anyway, I was speaking of the opportunity . . . I knew I would not see my mother and father again. During the three days and three nights I spent with them, I could not sleep or leave the house even to get a little fresh air. The outside world had turned into the most dangerous place. One of those cats, dogs, and maybe—no, not maybe, certainly—one of those human beings would one day discover my parents, trap and tear them to pieces. Either eat them or toss them into the soil and obliterate them. Say none of this happened, their tired hearts would still just give up from living day after day with so much fear. I wouldn't find them alive, even if I tried to visit again . . .
>
> So I decided not to return home without first wandering around a little. In fact, the night when I left our nest, I had walked to the avenue in front of us instead of trekking through the back lots. This way, I extended my trip by half a night. I was supposed to reach my mother's nest before the moon was out, but I arrived at dawn, suffering sharp pains flashing through my eyes straight to my

heart. I was oblivious to the dangers I managed to escape near their nest, but they—with their hearts pulsing inside their mouths—they embraced me, and wept and wept. There had been humans on the road, cars that suddenly appeared and disappeared, lights that blinded and dazed me, noises . . . I had wandered quite a while along that avenue, but in the end, realizing that this wasn't for me after all, I had walked along the trees, the shrubbery and the fences, to reach my mother. But I didn't want to take the same path back, definitely not the avenue. Both because I was frightened by that grand expanse and because I wanted to see other places. Yet, the porcupine can never know where danger really lies. Where you think it does, nothing happens, yet the place you've known as your mother's nest turns out to be surrounded with creatures waiting in line to kill you. So I decided I would take different streets, see my enemies one by one, and learn to recognize them. If they attacked and killed me, I wouldn't see you again. And you would then have to fend for yourselves. Of course, I wouldn't court danger deliberately . . . I would be cautious. Defend myself and even fight but only if confronted with certain death . . .

For us porcupines, life in this world is quite difficult. It must be easier for others. Certainly, dogs or cats have no such worries. Who would attack them? Whom couldn't they escape from? Then again, as porcupines, we don't know everything there is to know about such matters . . .

Why would I lie? In one of my grandfather's fairy tales, there was a place called "the sea." Presumably, it was like water and it began where the land ended. Not that my grandfather had seen it personally, he knew about it through the fairy tales passed down from his grandfather, his grandfather's grandfather. Of course, it was crazy. How would I have seen something that no one else had seen before? Besides, had there been a sea around, the travelers would have told us. Crazy, yes, but one still hopes . . . of course I never discovered it. And gave up thinking that I ever would. Still, I tell it to my grandchildren, saying that I heard it from my grandfather. Perhaps one of them, or one of their grandchildren, will one day get to the sea. One never knows.

Anyway, to make it short. The cars kept appearing and disappearing . . . One had to avoid getting too close to them, I figured out that much. Nothing can be done against them. So I chose the less traveled streets. While walking by a wall, I was accosted by three humans. I have my quills, like all porcupines. I rolled myself into a ball and swelled up. These humans must have been big since they didn't seem threatened by my quills. Prodding me with a stick, they managed to turn me on my back. I escaped but was caught again. Their mouths are very small and, besides, stand much too high above the ground. How they would manage to eat me, I couldn't tell. I recalled my mother's story. Would they just rip me to pieces and leave? And there were three of them. Three great big bodies—what part of me could satisfy their hunger? Either they would fight each other to eat me, in which case I would be able to escape, or they would kill and toss me aside. And that would be the end of the sorry ordeal . . . But they just kept prodding me and nothing else. Perhaps my quills are still good for something, I thought to myself. I was puzzled. Then came some shouts. My assailants retreated. Now a man was standing in front of me; he must have been the one shouting. He must have scared the others away. "That's it," I thought to myself, "this one will eat me." I'd been expecting the others to fight over me, but now a new person had appeared, and his mouth was much too close for comfort. The others had flipped me on my back and left. I was still struggling. What if I pretended to be dead? Would he change his mind about eating me? Do they prefer eating us alive or dead, how would I know? What if this human being was one of those who just killed and abandoned their victim? Since he scared the others away, he would have to be very strong. I waited. I could feel my heart pulsing inside my mouth. He didn't move. He would suddenly pounce, I was convinced, he was gathering strength, getting ready. Terrified, I flung myself off the edge of the wall, rolled over and ran.

Somewhat later, I stopped and considered. That man had not attacked me right away, but not because he couldn't eat me. Instead, I concluded, because he didn't like porcupines: And that's also why he didn't let the others eat me either. You know the type who says, I would neither eat maggots—even if you kill me—nor let you eat them. He was like that . . .

Since then I have wandered around much but, quite frankly, avoided human beings. Not all of them want to kill porcupines, that much is clear. And some among them don't like porcupines altogether. What I'm trying to say is that not everyone is our enemy. But who is and who isn't, how can you tell?

I have quills, that's how I am. When approached, I roll myself into a ball. Cats, dogs, human beings, it makes no difference. But human beings, I can't figure them out—their claws are hidden, or maybe they don't have any, and they are also very self-possessed. That's also why I can never predict what they will do next, why I am petrified when I run into them. Somewhere on their bodies, they must have a secret weapon, a lash or quills, although I can't tell where. All I can say is that, when approached, I roll myself into a ball and erect my quills; that's all I know, all I know for certain. That's the way we porcupines are. That's how we are born, and that's how we die. Even if we live long enough, all that we ever learn, I think, is to erect our quills neither too soon nor too late. You probably haven't forgotten our old neighbor who used to say that you must wait before erecting your quills and determine first whether the caller is a friend or an enemy, anything else is uncivilized behavior. I also had started believing him. Oddly enough, I still continue to believe, despite what happened early last winter. As far as I am concerned, his blood-covered body hanging between the jaws of that monster does not disprove his theory. Yes, perhaps he erected his quills too late, his timing might have been off; but the monster, as you will agree, resembled no creature we know; it must have come from the outside since we never saw it again, nor anything like it . . . That monster, as I was saying, was perhaps more ferocious and cunning than any of our known enemies. As porcupines, we ought to be prepared, but we also ought to heed our neighbor's words and stop perceiving the entire world as our enemy. Do we have friends? We don't know. Why? Because we haven't even bothered to find out. No matter who approaches us . . . I've already said it . . . Well, right now I am in no state to answer this important question. But I do know one thing; we ought to be less fearful. And to be less fearful, we ought to travel, face real danger and learn how to overcome it. When I first left home, I thought I'd only encounter enemies, but I also encountered friends. Will we always find the time needed to recognize a friend? I know: we don't have that much time. Then again, a dog and I walked together the entire length of a street. First it came over and sniffed, my quills pricked its nuzzle. It stopped. I extended my head and looked. It didn't attack me. I walked, it walked. Then it ran ahead, then waited for me to catch up. Another time, I did the same things with a cat. Though for half the length of a street. What I am saying is, they don't always attack. I had taken to the road in defiance of my enemies, but I also learned that you can find friends. It's all a matter of timing.

I was quite irritated by this porcupine's chattiness. True, it was saying certain things worth hearing . . . Yet, it had become so very garrulous. I was surprised. If it could become this talkative just by thinking that it had grown wiser . . . I didn't want to know any more. I chased the porcupine away from my mind, kept it out for a long while. Yet little by little I came to understand its chattiness. Just returned from the journey, it had experienced plenty, so it was excited; before it hadn't been living at all, and it had suddenly started experiencing life to the fullest. Yet, once the excitement passed, did the porcupine find anything else among the dregs of emotions? Did it gain any new insight?

I listened again to my porcupinity. It had grown a little old, my porcupine; the tips of its quills had turned gray. It had gathered its grandchildren around, and was talking to them. I lent an ear to my porcupinity:

> I saw very different places, ate very different insects, smelled different smells. The earth was soft in places, hard in others; we already know as much,

you may say. Nor do I think I'm saying anything
new. Only that I lived through this. That I hope
you live through it as well . . . No need to bela-
bor the point, I thought I should end my travels
and take the shortest cuts to return here. Your
mother, your father, and your brother, they were
all young back then . . . I learned what fear is.
And I experienced enough to know pretty well
what to be afraid of. As a consequence I felt a kind
of fearlessness. After that journey, I stopped going
anywhere. Nor will I ever leave again. On this plot
of land, wandering around it, I will await death. If
any one is looking for me—friend or enemy—let
him come and look for me here, on this soil. This
is my homeland, this is where we fight, this is
where we shake hands. I feel less lonely here, here
I know better, perhaps . . .

The porcupine must have spoken thus.

1968–1969

"Fear became my life's only passion,"
Hobbes supposedly said . . .
If the attribution or the translation
is not incorrect, it's interesting.

IN PRAISE OF THE CRAB

For Cüneyt Türel

I could say it like this:

My friend must have realized that I noticed the crab standing on the little table.

—Have I ever told you the story of this brave crab? he asked. When I told him that we have never talked about crabs or, for that matter, about bravery until today, he lifted the shell of the crab. What I thought was a metal crab statuette painted in black turned out to be a masterfully crafted box; inside it was the lower pincer of a crab's claw. . . .

My friend closed the lid, and started to tell . . .

It may well turn out to be something different, you never know. Narratives like this used to be popular a hundred years ago, but I may still please quite a number of readers who think, even today, that this is the only writing form that "narrates" something. Yet, can you turn back the clock so easily?

Or I could also say it like this:

Cuneyt shut the lid of the crab-shaped metal box. In those days, banners hung across the streets and on the façades of buildings, banners that displayed Cancer Week slogans: words bracketed on both ends with large images of crabs . . . Slogans that had long lost their meaning because they were repeated countless times and never rephrased . . . Is it too expensive to find new words?

Does each repetition weaken the word? We can ask the opposite: Does each repetition strengthen the word? We should talk about this when we are together.

The new is always true, it is new *and* true. The venerable experts of the past used to perceive this as an axiom not even worth arguing about. What makes the new new? We should talk about this also . . .

It was thirty-five years ago. My teacher was describing cancer to me. "It's something like a crab," he was saying, "little by little, it eats away one's lungs, one's stomach. . . ." At that age, I didn't know the extent to which an image could lie. And besides, I loved eating crab. Yet, there were always baby crabs along the shore, some I caught with my fishing-line, some I missed, some I set on the dock (ignoring the reproach, "Leave it alone; toss it back in the sea") then returned to the sea with the flick of my finger.

And I could say it like that, too. Follow the lines of a fairly conventional narrative under a new name, and make plenty of people scoff at me.

A former student of mine came by the other day. He had a dream about me. Apparently I was holding a book with a brown cover. It was my own book. Translated into French. He could still remember the title: *Pauvre Mort* . . . What do you think? Should I write a book to go with that title now? About a dead crab being swept away . . .

On the meat-and-fish stand, the whiteness of the plastic container accentuated the murky water in it. Somehow the crab endured, but it was obviously dying in agony. The animal itself was primarily responsible for the dirt in the water. Its mouth kept moving. Coarse and sluggish, it stood like a rock in the water. "Why won't you give it something to eat," I reproached the children. "It's going to die anyway," they responded, "even if we gave it something it won't eat." I insisted. They were cleaning mackerels; they tossed in a few pairs of gills. Suddenly, it started to work, like a frightening little machine. At once it grabbed and devoured the gills. It didn't eat the third pair. Its dried-out shell has been hanging on the display case for days. I looked again today. Why this flawless showdown between the crab and death?)

• • •

The sun is in the sign of Cancer.

> (That is, in your hand. Or in your house. And how it befits you!)

The sun is in the sign of Cancer. The crab is under the stone. Under the rock, underneath, underneath. And Cuneyt is over the rock. That's all.

> (The title, "In Praise of the Crab," should have been placed here. Yet I followed custom and placed it at the beginning of the narrative—so it matched "In Praise of the Fearless Porcupine." Cuneyt told me about this experience two years ago. It was in the month of January. When the sun was in the house of the Ram, that is, in my hand.)

The sun is in the sign of Cancer, the crab under the stone.

The crab in question is from Kekova. A crab in the waters by the Arab Harbor, discovered because of its extraordinary size, then very skillfully pulled out by a diver, and set on the flat surface of a rock. A huge, dappled blue-green thing. People gather over it and stare; they hold it, the ones who are brave enough, that is. And Cuneyt is among them. Holding it in the place it can be held (*let's call it the waist; we should be able to call it so)* he picks it up. But for some reason—or an all-too-obvious reason—the crab is not enjoying being lifted in the air and watched. Tensely stretching its hind legs, it manages to find a way to scratch and bloody Cuneyt's wrist *(is it ever possible to think of Cancer, what we call 'hurt-me-not,' independently of blood?).* Its struggle is in vain, of course. A crab held like this can neither clutch its captor nor escape. But the crab is not using only its pincers to accomplish the impossible task; it's stretching its hind legs as far as possible, swinging them back, forth, sideways, any which way it can, in order to dissuade its captor. And it's emitting sharp angry sounds.

Cuneyt is not the kind of person who enjoys prolonging this anger and playing God; he releases the crab into the sea, and afterwards, lies down on the flat rock to bake his body in the sun.

He is lying on his belly. The sun is in the sign of Cancer. The crab is probably under the rock. Underneath it. Under the weight of the sun, Cuneyt is about to feel queasy.

All of a sudden, he hears the angry sounds nearby. *(Reckless gallantry is first experienced right here, I suppose.)* He opens his eyes, turns his head, and finds himself staring the crab in the eye *(we stare death in the eye, then why wouldn't we stare the crab in the eye?)* separated by just two spans. Literally, in the eye. Each terribly aware of the other. They stare. The crab continues to emit sharp, angry hisses; Cuneyt understands that the crab has come out of the water and climbed the rock for one reason: to strike him. The crab stands perfectly still, as if gathering speed, rage flexing its hind legs, its pincers. *(Is this bravery or impertinence? Is this meant to foolishly tempt the other to commit evil deeds? Then what's next? Strident complaints?)* Clearly, it will strike.

Cuneyt presses his palms against the rock and rises.

Now the crab stands on the spot where Cuneyt had previously laid his head.

One, from the peak of his height *(the peak is where the eye is)*, the other, from its width outspread one inch above the rock—they keep staring. The crab springs forward again. (Forward is Cuneyt; no returning any more. Cuneyt is the only direction in the universe.)

For Cuneyt, this is a conversation. A conversational showdown.

Facing the crab is its enemy. *(Is its enemy its choice or its choice an enemy?)* It must destroy him. The human standing before the crab is no longer a higher life form (he cannot be); the crab's choice has consented to being the enemy.

> (They say that people born in your sign always want to be protected by someone, protected, favored, pampered . . . —Yes, even pampered . . . — And afterwards, they say, the Cancer will make every effort to strike the one who protects, favors, pampers them; they will create opportunities, invent excuses if necessary, just to strike . . .)

Cuneyt will try to fight in a spirit of equality *(that is, brute, raw animal equality)*. Otherwise, the crab seems bent on suicide or—synonymously—calling up its own murder.

The crab, according to Cuneyt's account, seems very upset, very hurt about something done not by others but by Cuneyt in particular.

Mortal combat alone can redeem a crab's humiliated pride. The size of the enemy is immaterial. One or the other must die.

> (One Cancer tactic, they say, is to tire you out, to exhaust and exasperate you; to constantly expect that you put up with their whims. What does such behavior get them?)

The crab gets shoved off with a stick, thrown back into

the sea. Those gathered around Cuneyt try mightily to persuade the crab against its insane venture. The young boatman—the one who had dived and brought the crab out of the water—favors finishing off the crab by crushing it with a club. (I created it; I can destroy it. This is something that everyone, writer and savage alike, perceives as a fundamental right. Can we easily call it "wrong"?) But the others restrain the young boatman.

The crab reappears again on the spot where it was shoved and thrown in the water. *(Perhaps it is a little disoriented. Or is this too much of a human interpretation?)* Again, again it singles out Cuneyt in the crowd and makes clear that it is ready, that it is determined to strike him. *(Is this an attempt to conceal its lack of self-confidence?)*

(You're probably tired already . . . The Cancer, they say, will exasperate you not with their thoughts but with their actions, that's how they push people away, alienate them. They try to conceal their lack of self-confidence by being reckless. Yet why should they lack self-confidence? At the least, in appearance—*yet in appearance, only in appearance . . . After all, their thick shell ought to be good for something*—there is no reason why they should.)

From the human angle, the showdown begins to look more and more like a thirst for self-destruction.

When the crab again singles out Cuneyt in the crowd, and darts toward him, the boatman's club descends on its back with a loud cracking sound, and creates a depression as wide as the club on the shell. That dappled blue-green back is no more. Cuneyt appears full of sadness for having failed to scream in time to prevent the boatman's action. His hands, his feet, his face bear all the signs of remorse.

The crab is now in the water. Under a broken sun, in a hollow beneath a rock. A small wave flows in and out, in and out of the hole. The crab remains submerged. Between the crab and the eyes of the onlookers, the water rises and gurgles, and then recedes, becoming translucent: the movement seems like a play to the onlookers. *(Who wonders about the crab then?)* Yet this wavelet serves as a messenger to the world beyond the crab. A messenger of life-and-death. It spreads the odor of death everywhere, announces to the living the share of the living; it summons colonies of hungry tiny cyanea out of their hollows, from underneath the rocks.

The tiny creatures encircle the crab, striking in twos and threes. With its last proud defiance, the crab thrashes about, struggling to drive them away, to keep them off, unaware that it is emitting—incessantly, increasingly—the odor of mortal flesh that lures them to itself.

(In the case of suicide by one's own hand *(one can also commit suicide by the hand of another . . . I've often mentioned that film to you; Valerian Borowczyk's* Blanche *is a good example of what I am talking about)* if the act is to bear any value, it shouldn't be performed secretly, masked, or staged as an accident, delirium or desperation. Whether brief or elaborate *(Drieu La Rochelle comes to mind)*, a reason must be given before one attempts the act. *(Let's recall Kirilov in* The Possessed, *besides the many real writers, artists, intellectuals—that is, those who have lived in the company of people, those seen by the eyes, touched by the hands of others.)* Nermi Uğur was saying one day: "Choosing suicide means falling captive to a closed circuit. Yet, living means keeping the circuit, all circuits, open, ready for change, at all times. . . ." I'm not sure; can one not renounce, together with life, the open circuit also? Can one not transcend remorse, openness, freedom, with this final, irreversible act that obliterates all freedom?)

The crab *(couldn't give any reason. Perhaps because it wasn't human. In Cuneyt's words, its "bruised pride," or objec-*

tively speaking, its "aggression," cannot count as reason . . . Even humans are difficult to understand) is now disintegrating while it struggles within the swarm of cyanea that throbs like an immense, effusive heart. At least, that's how we see it from our angle.

In the end, the crab's wish gets fulfilled.

Cuneyt's heart cannot allow the tiny creatures to consume the crab shred by shred, fiber by fiber.

He leaps and as soon as he pulls the crab out of the water, he crushes it, tears it apart, smashes it under his bare soles.

He tears it apart, crushes it, smashes it, and throws it back in the water. Cuneyt. The crab. The little cyanea would still satisfy their hunger, yes, but their orgy is over. At the most, they will fight for scraps among themselves.

Cuneyt separates one of the lower pincers, and takes it as a keepsake.

• • •

So that was the story of the pincer inside the crab-shaped, black, metal box.

1973/1975

5.

A new movie had opened. I thought of going to the sweet shop and eating an ice cream after the movie. When I saw him going that way, I returned to my hotel room instead and went to bed.

Next morning, I toured the remaining sites, ate a light meal at a small restaurant, and went to the garden behind the ancient palace that the guide books recommended. The three fountains, the hedged paths, the grand pool with the water jet, all lived up to the elegant descriptions in the books. I sat under a tree and read a little. I must have fallen asleep.

He was behind a tree, staring at me. The tree stood in front of me. It was some kind of oak, but because its leaves were high above me, or perhaps because I was still half-asleep, I couldn't say for sure that it was an oak.

He wasn't smiling but laughing outright as he came out and walked toward me. His eyes were green, shining. He had a dried stalk of foxtail hanging from the corner of his mouth.

When he came near me, he plucked off the bristly ear, put it in my hair, and sat down. He continued to chew the end of the stalk. His green shirt was unbuttoned. Among the dark chest hair, a miniature silver greyhound

    or a roe deer

    or some other animal sitting with its long legs folded under its body

    tarnished, was hanging at the end of his necklace.

    When he noticed I saw it, he laughed again. He started to pick at the seeds and thorns that had clung to his trousers.

    "What I love best about this garden is that you can see the incessant running of water even in the pools," *he said.*

    There was no breeze. No sound of rustling leaves or grass. Everything looked green. Fall colors had not reached the garden yet.

    He sounded as though reciting by heart the sentence I had read in the guide book before coming here:

    "In the mid-eighteenth century, during the renovation that gave the front courtyard of the palace its current shape, a special arena was built for 'the Game of Departure,' in the garden behind the palace.

    "One of the rules required the overlord to sit in front of the palace and direct the players. In view of this, a special extension was added at the back of the palace . . ."

    His last sentences were not in the book. Perhaps I had read and forgotten them. Yet his voice was the voice he had last night at the café when he told

    when he began to tell

    the story of the game. Cold, as if reading from a book.

    But I had not heard these last details before.

    "For the last two hundred years, the game has been played not in the front courtyard but still across from the palace. You haven't seen the field yet. Then again, if you won't take part, it makes little difference if you see it or not."

    It was like I had forgotten that I was angry at him, since last night I didn't want to see him. I was listening, smiling. The only thing I managed to say was, "I will take part."

I got up, walked away without looking back. I walked in the direction where I presumed the game field was located. Shortly thereafter, I found myself facing a large clearing. The field was smaller than I had envisioned. The chess squares, two or three feet on each side, started in the outer circle and became smaller and smaller in the inner circles. I went and stood in a black marble square located in the second row. In the place of a pawn. I raised my head; he was standing in the Vizier's square, in the outermost circle.

"You resisted quite a bit," he said, "but, see, now you are in the game."

I stared at him. We were not smiling.

I went back to the tree and lay down.

When I woke up, it was getting dark.

THE SVN-MAN
OF THE RAINY CITY

To Ash, on her sixth birthday

A tiny, spindly, thirsty man was standing behind the closed window, its glass streaked with water. To a person looking in from the outside, his face appeared fluid, rippling. He gazed fixedly at the sky. Yet there was nothing worth seeing in the sky.

Absolutely nothing. Because in this land, it rained day and night, dawn to dusk. Rain that knew no rest or pause, no downpour or drizzle, just a steady rain that fell like strings of hair, like endless filaments. What was there to look at in that lead-hued changeless sky? What was there to see?

Because it rained, the asphalt avenues and cobblestone streets always glistened brilliantly, the walls were always clean but assumed a brooding countenance with mustachio-like streaks of soot running down the corners of window frames, while the red-tiled roofs always looked recently waxed and polished. If left alone, the gardens would have been luscious green, but—how could they?—the rain weighed down the smoke from the chimneys and laid it over the green like a blanket.

From cradle to grave, the inhabitants of the city knew only a monochrome sky, a monochrome sea, and if they ever learned that the sky could be blue—light, dark, any shade of blue—that the sea could match the sky's color by donning every imaginable color—deep blue, light green, even crimson, purple or yellow—they learned it from those who had traveled and seen the world. And more, according to these travelers' accounts, other places had a yellow sky—yellowish, whitish, reddish—glowing dazzlingly during the day. At night, the moon and the stars of myriad kinds filled up those skies. As for those who never left the city, they had seen no sun, no moon, no stars . . . True, they did learn in school that the sun was the source of daylight. Yet their day was lead-colored, or more precisely, a dreary leadish color—like their sky, like their sea.

The people in this city saw color only on the boats. The rowboats, barges and ships were painted yellow, crimson, green, blue, purple, every imaginable and unimaginable color, and then set off to sea.

Because it rained endlessly, the cats, the dogs, and especially the chickens seldom if ever wandered outside. Why on earth would they want to wander? To get soaked, fur and feather? To be sure, some of the cats, dogs and chickens lacked good sense and wandered out, got soaked, then became sick and bedridden. Only the geese enjoyed strolling in the rain. In flocks of tens and twenties, they walked with their wings and tails touching one another, resembling puffy clouds with legs floating just above the ground. And above the clouds, the long necks swayed like poplars, and the beaks, almost as if unconnected to the necks, opened and closed incessantly. Still, the flocks of geese were a rare sight, while there were plenty of down-hearted dogs and cats who sat forlorn under the awnings, against the walls . . .

In this city, people always carried umbrellas on the streets, and because these umbrellas were never closed, the main streets seemed forever canopied by a long billowy sheet stretched between the sky and the earth. This sheet would be tugged, tightened, swallowed only at the doors of the buses, trolley cars, houses and stores, as if being squeezed between mechanical lips, jaws, and cylinders . . .

Again because it rained endlessly, all the houses had nooks for wet umbrellas and shoes, and small gullies to drain these nooks.

More importantly, waking up in the morning was not the same as in other cities. Neither excited nor anxious about the weather, people did not rush to open the shutters or the blinds to check out the sky; or lying in bed, nobody thought to look for a ray of light that might be streaming between the curtains and reflecting on the wall, or to listen to the automobile tires to guess if it was raining or snowing, dry or sunny outside. The inhabitants knew that it was raining and so they neither looked nor listened. Nothing had ever changed since they were born . . .

Neither hope nor disappointment about the weather ever visited the people in this city. Met by the pouring rain when leaving the cinema, the theatre, the café or the concert hall, they never had to wait under the awnings or run home because they had forgotten their umbrellas. Nor did they ever think to themselves, if the weather is nice on Sunday, we can go to the beach, the soccer game, the park. They never anticipated anything like this . . .

No one knew the fear of being caught in the rain or waited for the skies to clear, except for one person. This man, this man standing behind the window, gazing fixedly at the sky . . . This man was alone. He worked in a tall office building in the city's business district; he went there in the morning and came back in the evening, never ask-

ing anyone to his house. He knew no one would come.
Nor did he visit friends or family, unless he was invited
time after time. A quiet man, he never hurt or offended
anyone. He only had one shortcoming. And for this reason, for this reason alone, his family and friends were
weary of him.

True, he had not left the city to see the world or any
other skies, but he had read about the sun and listened to
the travelers' accounts. On the rare occasion when he
broke his customary silence and began to say, "Tomorrow
morning," everyone invariably responded, "Yes, yes . . ."
and walked away from him. Because they knew what
would follow, even though for this very reason he seldom
got to finish his sentence.

"Tomorrow morning, suppose you saw the sun in the
sky. What would you do?" And that's all he would say any-
how. If they let him say it . . .

So he was obsessed. What if the sun appeared, what if
it showed itself . . . Yet everyone knew what it meant to
see the sun. It meant the rain would stop, the clouds
would clear, the same old sky they had known since the
day they were born would change, the umbrellas, the drying nooks would fall into disuse, and still worse, they
would experience hope and disappointment. It meant the
stones, the walls and the red tiles would dry out and lose
their sheen, and the smoke would rise to the sky instead of
descending on the green. Could all this be possible?

Were it not for his disagreeable fixation, his friends
and acquaintances would certainly have shown more
affection toward him; instead, they enjoyed no peace of
mind, expecting all the time his words, "Tomorrow
morning . . ."

The man returns home, bathes, brushes his teeth, goes to
bed; he reads books, smokes cigarettes, then falls asleep.

But whenever this habitual grayish lead—or leadish

gray—color becomes light, flows into his room, and brings him the news that morning has arrived . . .

He can't help it. Knowing well that it is sheer madness, he still gets out of bed, walks to the window, and looks at the sky through the rain-streaked glass.

On his face—on his fluid, rippling face seen from the outside, by someone who neither finds a trace of curiosity nor a trace of hope on this face—only his eyes seem alive. He looks at the sky, thinking that perhaps the sun has risen today. And if not today, there is always tomorrow, the day after tomorrow. But when he stands in front of the window, this is what he absolutely knows: The sun will not rise today either, it will not show itself . . .

Yet, if even while lying in bed he had not noticed any change in the light, then how come he imagines that, once he goes to the window, he will see the sun? We have already established: This poor man is a bit odd, a bit peculiar . . . Even without allowing hope to show on his face—and a little foolishly—he keeps nursing it in his heart . . .

1968

6.

*I entered the restaurant below the hotel, and he was sitting
at the same table as on the first evening. I, too, sat where I had
sat then. His back was again turned toward me.*

*That evening I had not noticed the mirror. It was long and
narrow. In it, I saw he was looking at me. Perhaps he was angry
at me. His face was icy cold. I lowered my eyes. When I got up, he
was still sitting. The next day and the day after next, somehow
we didn't see each other.*

*In truth, I had planned my trip to coincide with the game. I
certainly wasn't about to give up watching the game just because
I met a man who frustrated and confounded me with obscure
histories. For two days, hundreds of tourists materialized as if
sprouting from rocks and soil. There must have been no vacan-
cies anywhere, hotels or bed-and-breakfasts. The streets became
practically impassable. Everyone was talking about the game.
You could hear all kinds of facts and confabulations about it, if*

you stood long enough anywhere in town, be it a restaurant, café, street or alleyway.

Yet in this noisy tempest, I heard nothing that resembled his descriptions, as if this knowledge was based on sources entirely different. Or fabricated.

In a way, I shouldn't have been surprised that he was nowhere to be seen. He who knows what he knows,

whether truth or fabrication,

would certainly not mix with people

so self-assured about what they know when they know
    more or less

the same information

Even I feel superior at times and tend to look with pity at the herd of tourists. . . .

I checked with the porters at the hotel. They told me I didn't need a ticket to watch the game. Thanks to the rows and rows of bleachers skillfully set up on the steps surrounding the game field

(long long before the games,

long before the wafer wheels, the legendary sweets,

these steps must have been the special feature of the town)

that could comfortably accommodate four thousand spectators, all that one had to do was show up and find a free seat.

The number of spectators seemed to me already around ten thousand, although the town's small size, more exactly, its narrowness, may account for my over-estimation.

"If you arrive an hour before the game, you should be fine . . ." said the porter. "You would find not just a seat but a good seat. In any case, there is something the tourists don't know.

(even though he knew I was a tourist as well, he treated me differently from the rest probably because I could speak his native language as well as he)

"They rush to get seats in the front rows and pile on top of each other. Yet the best places to sit are around the game-master

"as you know, in the old days, the town's feudal lord would direct the game, but in the last hundred years, the mayors have

*taken his place, and consequently, each mayor spends the weeks
and months prior to the game diligently working to learn from
the former mayor all that needs to be learned about the game.
It's like a secret art being passed from father to son, they say. I
don't know. Those who want to believe believe since, as you
know, people love to invent mysteries just to arouse your curiosity, where was I, oh, yes,*

*"around the mayor, that is, in the highest, the very last two
rows. I'd suggest you sit there."*

*The game was tomorrow. I had seen all the sites. I took my
book along and spent the entire day at the café on the hill overlooking the ancient palace. I sat at the table where he and I had
first talked. He didn't show up. I finished reading a newspaper,
two magazines and a book. I went to dinner, then to a movie,
and decided to go back to my room early to recover from the fatigue of sitting all day. At the hotel, I greeted the doorman with
a smile. He stopped me. He wasn't smiling. With visible
gravity, he handed me an envelope. "It's from the Mayor's Office; they delivered it just now."*

*My name was written on the envelope. I was surprised and
felt slightly anxious when opening it. The letter was handwrit-
ten. It had the embossed seal of the town's council. Below the
writing was a waxed seal as well. The mayor's signature was in
dark red ink.*

"As you know," *started the letter*, "our town's traditional
game involves thirty-two players; only ten players of the
Purple team are selected from among our town's people,
and by the ten Purple players who played in the previous
game. According to tradition, the player in each square
must be of a certain age, and consequently, the selection
requires meticulous calculations. Notices posted around
town solicit the remaining twenty-two players. We have
been able to fill twenty-one positions with volunteers who
met the age requirements.

"One of our foreign players informed us that your
age matched that of the vacant position. We had hoped

that you would personally volunteer and waited until this evening. Please accept our apologies for the disrespect we commit in inviting you by letter. However, please also note that, once invited, you cannot choose not to participate in the game.

"We thank you in advance. Before you take your place as the middle pawn with the Purple team, we request that you meet us tomorrow morning at 8:00, in the Lord's Hall in the Palace, to receive your special instructions."

I had not read such a letter before. The doorman was anxiously staring at me. "Green or Purple?" he simply asked. "Purple," I replied. "May God help you," he said, "do whatever it takes to be captured quickly so you don't remain in the field until the end." He turned and left. I watched him disappear. Then I went upstairs to sleep.

facilis descensus Averni; noctes atque dies patet atri janua Ditis; Sed revocare gradum, superasque evadere ad auras, hoc opus, hic labor est.

The descent to Avernus is easy; the gate of Pluto stands open night and day; but to retrace one's steps and return to the upper air, that is the toil, that the difficulty.

Virgil

THE MAN WALKING
IN THE TUNNEL

At the mention of the sea, the currents that flow in every direction couldn't hold back, joining together and heading toward a shore—sandy or pebbly . . .

The young man couldn't hold back—he is so in love with the sea. Lying on the pebbles, stretching his body on the surface of the sea, crawling through the currents, sprawling out on the sand . . . For him, living means going to the sea in the summer, and waiting in the winter for the sea.

The summer he turns nineteen, he goes to the sea again. To a pebbled beach on a rocky island . . . The air seems particularly vibrant, and the sea reflects the sun's full heat as in a mirror. He swims, stretches on the pebbles, tanning himself, and when he rises and puts on his clothes, he doesn't walk back right away, deciding instead to stroll along the shore for a while. At the end of the beach, he comes upon a huge rubble heap, the remains of a hilltop that must have fallen down to be crushed and crumbled by the sea. He experiences a strange feeling. There is no path through. Yet he very much wants to cross to the other side. How? A man with common sense would not have kept trying, and if he had to, he would have turned back, walked up the gravel slope past the highway, climbed the hill that rose just above the cliff, and searched for a path beyond this vein of rock descending from the hill to the sea. If he found it, fine, if he didn't, he would have returned just as he had come, and descended to the anchorage behind the hill. But this particular young man obviously lacks common sense. Not that he is lazy; rather he dismisses common sense and reasonable behavior as unnecessary limits . . . The only path, he decides, is crossing by way of the sea. He rolls up his pants, takes off his shoes, holds them in his hand, and walks into the sea. Between the rocks, the water is quite deep, and falling in one of the gaps would mean getting soaked, but he carefully leaps and skips from rock to rock, trying to avoid jagged edges as much as possible; even so, his feet are sore and bleeding by the time he reaches the farthest rock and climbs it. He takes a deep breath. He is exhausted by all the acrobatics. He has tied his towel around his neck, but holding on to his shoes is quite troublesome. Now he can see the other side of the cliff.

And he realizes that up until this point, the rocks have lined up like stepping-stones; his ordeal hasn't been as significant as it has seemed . . . At first, the thought of turning back crosses his mind, but he feels ashamed for thinking it. He removes his belt and uses it to tie his shoes and his towel together; he hangs the bundle over his shoulder, and grips the tip of the belt between his teeth. He carefully climbs down the rock; just below the water's surface, there is a narrow ledge where he rests his feet.

Nothing but water extending all the way to the shore, and the cliff-face in front of him as flat as a wall—not a single knob he could grasp or step on. The shore is eighty to ninety feet away, he can see the small beach with fine, shimmering sand . . . But no one could reach this spot since it's surrounded by rock walls, smooth, as if polished. The only access, if it could be said to be one, is by sea, far too deep for walking. If he leaves his clothes on the rock and swims to shore, he could lie in the sun a little more, but he would still have to swim back, and besides, the slightest breeze would sweep his clothes into the sea. The young man feels disheartened, he has no choice but to give up.

But is that true? Just as he is turning his head, he notices behind him a narrow opening where the sea meets the wall-like cliff facing the rock he is standing next to— an opening that resembles a cave entrance. It certainly is a cave entrance; it seems to be smiling darkly, and the young man smiles back. I'll go in and see, he thinks, if it looks like there might be an underground path leading up to the hill, I'll move forward, and if not, I'll turn back; what's the harm in trying?

Entering through the hole proves a little difficult. His backside and his pant legs get wet as he squats down, and the water is somewhat deep. But once inside, he can stand upright. Even though he is tall, the rock ceiling spreads four spans above his head. The ground is cold, and when he is certain the tunnel is dry, he pulls his shoes out of the bundle and wears them. He carries his towel, still tied with the belt, on his shoulder. He turns back and looks. Now the mouth of the tunnel stands at a considerable distance. Yet light is still streaming in. This puzzles him. He looks again. The light is coming from nowhere else. Strange! After walking a little further, he notices on the wall— illuminated by the light streaming through the opening— lines that resemble letters. He approaches, looking intently: yes, the letters spell "DO NOT ENTER" on the wall. The lines have faded—it must have been written a long time ago. "Did the municipality post this?" the young man thinks and laughs to himself; he shrugs and continues to walk.

Leaving home, riding the ferry, disembarking, getting to the pebbled beach . . . he has forgotten everything; he has only one thought: to walk to the end of this tunnel . . . It would either open to a cave or lead him to another part of the island; or like blind alleys, it would abruptly end, in which case the young man would turn around and walk back. Even if the tunnel spans the entire length of the island, finding its exit, its other end, couldn't take more than two hours.

Sometime later, he thinks he sees a faint light ahead of him. He hastens his steps. He's right; light is flowing in. He turns and looks back; no light is coming from that end. He has been walking on a straight path, he has turned no corners, nor has he noticed any curves along the way. The tunnel could not have circled back toward the cave's mouth. Best to walk toward the light, he thinks.

The bright point draws nearer and nearer, and soon he discovers much to his surprise that it is not a source of light at all. A steel panel bolted to the rock reflects light coming from much farther away. In the faint light, his eyes discern another inscription on the wall next to the steel mirror: "WISH YOU DIDN'T ENTER." He finds this vexing. He is willing to grant that the municipality might have posted the first message. But this one must have been written by someone with a penchant for tasteless jokes. But what about the steel panel? The mirror? Who mounted that mirror there? Besides, if the municipality deemed the tunnel dangerous, then it would have fenced off the entrance and rid itself of the problem.

His mind grows restless: he has to walk, move forward, and find where the light is coming from—an exit, a door, an air hole, whatever it is.

He walks, walks in the faint light.

He feels tired, checks his watch, it is twelve o'clock.

He entered the tunnel long past the noon hour. But it can't be midnight; he hasn't walked for that long. Besides, he can see ahead of him, very far ahead of him, another faint glow. Another mirror or not, it means that it is still daylight outside, he thinks. But he is too tired to walk. He sits down. The ground is not cold here; the air is somewhat warm, too.

He wakes up with a start. As if someone has nudged him. He looks around. After the darkness of sleep, his surroundings have become more discernible. He checks his watch. It still shows twelve. He tries to wind it, but the watch-spring feels tight, as if recently wound. He rises to his feet and begins to walk.

He feels hungry as always when he wakes up. And not just a little. Hungry as a wolf. His frustration is mounting. This is taking entirely too long. Besides, when he lay down to sleep, he lost his sense of direction. Even if he wants to go back, he can not determine which way to turn. He has no choice but to walk toward the faint but still visible light.

He is upset. And hungry. Something has to happen, he has to find the end of the path. Or else . . . Or else, he keeps saying but can't complete his thought. He isn't weary or afraid but . . .

After a long walk, he reaches the point of light. Just as he is about to say, "Another steel mirror," what he sees startles him. This one is not a mirror but a vending machine! One of those coin-operated machines that, when you push a button and move a lever, delivers a tray of food to the customer . . . Amused, he takes a quarter from his pocket, drops it in the slot, and moves the lever. The machine does not offer selections—strange that it operates on a quarter. Stranger still, the tray arrives carrying a clean, fresh sizzling plate of fried fish. Bread, salt, pepper, lemon wedges, forks and knives are available in plastic bags next to the machine.

"Figures!" says the young man, "It's a scheme to lure the tourists . . . And look . . ." He reads the instructions on his plate. *Discharge bones inside hole below. Deposit plate, fork and knife in box above machine. Pull lever in lower left corner.* He does everything as instructed. The hole sucks in the bones, and the box swallows the dishes. Nothing is mentioned about the bread slices. He slips the leftover slice in his pocket to eat when he gets hungry on the way.

But there are no tourists, there is no one, he is alone. He wonders whether the machine has ever served anyone else besides him.

His watch still shows twelve o'clock. It is working even though its spring is not unwinding.

Just then he remembers something. Something residual, faraway. Perhaps it is indeed faraway, this remembered moment. Does he know how long he has been walking down this tunnel? The duration, the hour, the day—isn't he confusing everything?

This is what he remembers: At the end of the shoreline, when he came upon the cliffs rising like a wall in front of him, he experienced a strange sensation. Now he is beginning to understand why. Having stared and stared at the perfectly level sea, the perfectly still horizon, he had almost forgotten that the world held another dimension. At the sight of the wall, this forgotten dimension had again become reality—one that, almost hitting him in the face, was as close as it was insurmountable and disheartening . . . Just now he is able to understand the sensation. Because the reality of having long been advancing through a dimensionless, desolate world is slowly rising into consciousness, taking shape in his mind, in his heart.

He smiles. "I am scared," he says. "If I weren't scared, I wouldn't smile at the thought. But since I can do nothing but keep walking . . ." He can think of no alternatives.

And there are no forks on the path to give him choices; he can only move forward, until he reaches the end, or— possibly—the beginning, the point where he had started, until he returns to the cave mouth that opened to the sea . . .

He is moving forward, and somewhere always ahead of him, there is the light. Vending machines, steel mirrors keep reflecting this light coming from somewhere. Each time he feels hungry, he comes upon a vending machine. The machines offer him enough food—never too little or too much—just enough to curb his hunger. One offers salted snacks, another sweets, another water, another *ayran*, another fish, another vegetables . . .

There are even cigarette machines. And once, shortly after he runs out of coins, he thinks "What's missing is a change machine." And pronto! He comes upon a change machine. Taking the two tens out of his pocket, he inserts them, and two pocketfuls of nickel coins come gushing out. But they are also spent along the way.

Measuring time by his hunger spells and the food he consumes, he seems to have been walking on this path for almost a year, but how could he know? A year or a week, he is in no condition to determine.

Whenever he feels sleepy, he makes certain to lie down face forward so as to keep his sense of direction. And his beard grows whenever he feels sleepy. But each time he wakes up and feels his face with his hand, he finds his skin as smooth as if just shaven.

On this path that knows neither night nor day, illuminated by a light that neither wanes nor waxes but reflects off the steel faces of vending machines, on this path where it is always twelve o'clock, there can be no morning or evening, no yesterday, today, or tomorrow . . . Besides, the young man has already forgotten these. He only knows one thing: walking. Why or how had he entered, he no longer remembers. Yet he knows why he is walking: to reach the light. And what will happen when he reaches the light? He does not know this either.

To reach the light . . . Not the light reflecting off the steel machines, but the true light . . .

What is the true light? From time to time the question gives him pause. He asks himself, yes, but he can't find an answer. What is it? What is its source? What will happen in the end? Eventually he reaches a point when he forgets even these questions, and from then on, he asks himself nothing . . .

He walks.

He has run out of money but now the vending machines dispense food without charge. To break the tedium of the unswerving path, he stops every so often and leans his hand against the wall; in time, he discovers that, at his touch, the walls billow, warp and curve. Then, little by little, they turn solid again.

He walks. The light is not much closer than before. It still reflects off the machines. Yet, his eyes have grown used to this darkness, and he carries on as if the tunnel were fully illuminated. But he knows the light is still ahead of him. And because he knows this, he is able to keep walking. He will reach the light.

All of a sudden, it occurs to him that there are fewer and fewer vending machines. For quite some time, he has been experiencing hunger so intense that he isn't able to stand on his feet, and, now falling, now dragging his body, he can barely reach the next machine. By the time he finds a water machine, his throat is parched, and his eyes throb with stabbing pains.

He decides to hasten his steps. Now he is almost running. But the next machine always seems farther and farther ahead.

"I am dying," he says at one point, "this path must have been laid out to kill people . . ."

He is not dying. He is running to escape death, running faster and faster.

Every so often, he stops to catch his breath. Then "I must run," he tells himself, "must keep running, must find the next machine before I die, before I'm exhausted. . . ."

He isn't even thinking about reaching the light any more. That thought will have to wait. For now he needs the machines. Machines. Nothing else. Or he will die.

Yet, the fewer the machines, the farther the distance between then, the stronger the light seems. He concludes this by the whiteness of his skin—his hands, his arms looking whiter and whiter. He can also recognize the machines by their dark silhouettes, rather than the light reflecting off them.

The walls have become solid again. The path stretches straight ahead, steadily gaining elevation. He can see the straight path with his own eyes, instead of feeling it with his feet. It means the light is growing much brighter. There are even fewer machines. So he runs and runs. But the more he is certain of the light, the true light, the less he thinks of the machines. He even skips one, running on to the next. Now the light is in sight. So is the end of the path. He could wager his life that it is.

But now, each time he wakes up from sleep and sees the light waiting at the end of the path, he begins to experience a strange nausea. A nausea not inside his body but inside his mind.

He sleeps and wakes up one more time. The light seems brighter still. Something else besides the light is streaming in. He recognizes it—fresh air, something like a breeze. He runs, runs, and runs. Now the breeze also ushers in a scent. At first he can't recognize it, but then, quite suddenly, he screams, "The scent of flowers!" His voice echoes through the tunnel. The voice he's forgotten. His sharp voice. Everything that had deserted his consciousness is now returning. People, strangers, crowds . . . He remembers bees. Bees crowding the flowers . . . Flies swarming over the sweet pastries . . . Birds perching on branches then flying away . . . Not having eaten or drunk for some time, he has stopped thinking about the machines. In the distance, a hole is growing steadily. It hurts his eyes; he keeps squinting. The light makes him notice the wrinkles forming over his ashy skin. He feels the widening hole pierce through his brain; "It's not the hole," he thinks in the end, "it's the light that's piercing through my brain . . ."

The wider the hole becomes, the less he can see. "Am I entering the darkness again?" he is frightened, "or could it be that what looks like a hole is just another object reflecting the light?" But it isn't. The fresh air, the breeze, the scents, the murmuring, every sensation is becoming more intense. The hole is real, the light is real. But why are his eyes failing?

He stops. Brings his hand to his forehead. Wants to rub off the pain lodged there. His fingertips feel moist— it's blood, probably. Warm, slippery, runny, oozing off the spot on his forehead that hurts the most. He must have run into the wall. He takes a step forward and stubs his foot against the wall. He must have fainted and hit the wall. But when he turns around, he cannot see the opposite wall. He moves his hand about and manages to touch it. He resumes walking toward the hole. He is not running any more. Beyond the clouds, beyond the streaks of smoke, the hole assumes a faint lifeless glow. So he is also beginning to remember the streaks of smoke, the clouds. But the hole is steadily diminishing before him.

Soon he no longer sees the hole. He realizes he has lost his sight. He stops. If he turns around and reenters the darkness, would his eyes see again? He has neither the heart not the strength to attempt a return . . . He is hungry, thirsty. His hand that's been feeling its way along the wall suddenly finds itself suspended in the void. There is no wall to his right or left. The wind beats against his face. The air is saturated with the scent of flowers, his ears are filled with the buzzing of insects. He must have passed through the hole. Emerged into the light.

He lifts his face. The sun is warm, spreading across his skin. From a distance comes the pulsing roar of the waves down below. His foot comes to rest against a surface. He feels it with his hand. A flat rock. He sits down. He lifts his face again. The warmth spreads from his face into his being. Yet deep inside, a spot remains ice-cold. The light's warmth cannot reach this spot. Seized by this warmth, this lightlessness, he is utterly alone, inside out.

"I suppose the dead begin to turn cold from inside out," he says. His beautiful—heartbreakingly beautiful—and youthful face turns skyward, his feet touch each other, his hands press tightly against the two sides of the rock, and he remains there, still.

1969

In August 1969, Ali Poyrazoglu described this:

> *A man caught a salt-water fish one day, he loved it so much that he wanted to keep it with him forever. Every day, he changed its water by carrying buckets and buckets from the sea. Eventually, he got tired of carrying seawater and tried tap water instead. At first, the fish was a little weary, but in the end, it got used to fresh water. Time came and passed, and the man began to wonder whether a fish that got used to fresh water could also get used to air . . . (If you ask me, the fish must have been either credulous or overly fond of the man—which itself can at times be a form of credulity. Let's return to Ali Poyrazoglu's tale.) The fish appeared asphyxiated at first, and*

struggled some, but soon enough, it got used to air as well. One day, the man decided he wanted to go to the sea. Together with his fish. He left the fish in a shady corner on the pebbled beach, and he went to swim. Children were passing by. They saw the fish. Somehow, they felt sorry for it. How sad, they said, the fish must have been beached, let's throw it back in the water. By the time the man could frantically swim back, the fish was already drowned in the sea.

On this matter, I will agree with Levi-Strauss's principle; in my opinion, the contrasts between these two tales are more significant than the similarities.

7.

My meeting with the mayor was brief. As soon as I asked how to find his office, the young attendant at the palace gate escorted me in, walking ahead of me. We walked for quite some time, passing through one hall after another. These areas of the palace were closed to tourists. I couldn't help but admire the tall ceilings, the elegant ornaments, the paintings. The young attendant seemed to walk slowly to give me time to look around. We came to a closed door which he opened without knocking. He respectfully bowed to a person I couldn't see, moved aside to let me proceed and, leaving, closed the door.

The mayor asked me to have a seat. He thanked me for coming and started to talk.

When I came out, the young attendant was waiting for me. We walked in a different direction and he took me through a back gate to the garden. The garden didn't look at all like the place I had visited three days ago.

Today the round arena looked much larger; and this time it was divided not into squares but into circles; they were marble but not black and white—green and purple instead, with yellow marble in between. The amazingly precise circles were over three feet in diameter and masterfully laid. The arena had just been washed and the colors glowed with a deep brilliance. Bleachers were built around the arena and already a few spectators had taken their seats, wearing paper hats and reading books and magazines. The game would start at eleven o'clock. It was now twenty past eight.

The young attendant escorted me back to the palace and showed me into a small room. Cushions were spread on a stone bench. My costume was lying on a five-hundred-year-old walnut armchair. "Rest a little, "he said. "I will lock your door and leave. I hope you won't mind—it's an old rule we've had for centuries. Before the game, the players cannot speak either among themselves or to others. I will come back at ten so you'll know when it's time to put on your costume." He walked out. The key turned three times inside the lock.

I was upset. All this was too much. But if I pounded on the door I'd only embarrass myself. I was angry at my own naïveté. If I hadn't gone to see the mayor, would they have dragged me here by force? So much for all the fine words about being courteous to visitors . . .

Then again, these people were willing to include me in one of the town's oldest rituals. If I didn't want to participate, nobody would force me to. I had feigned a lack of interest, almost convincing myself that I really didn't want to play. But in reality, didn't I jump at the chance when he asked me if I would take part in the game?

I lay down, must have fallen asleep. His head
this time a paler shade of chestnut
was touching mine. I felt the warmth of his lips on my ear.
"It was a dream," I said in the darkness of my closed eyes.
Then the room was illuminated again.
I saw his arm this time. I touched it, my fingertip caressing,

and then I jabbed his wrist with my finger. No blood appeared. He wasn't hurt. When I pulled my finger away, there was no trace on his wrist. His playful lips again found my ear, my cheek. A soft breeze filled the room.

I was in the dark again. "It was a dream," I repeated.

I opened my eyes. The door was open. The young attendant was calling me softly, gently squeezing my shoulder. I got up. "Please arrange your costume carefully, as you see it on this chart," he said.

Arranging these strange, unusual garments was not an easy task. Some pieces had to overlap, others were worn side by side. After putting on the seven-piece costume, I had fourteen more things to do.

I tied the Purple band around my waist. I tucked the wheat stalk in my knee pad, hung the pair of pliers over my shoulder; the small cleaver in its own sheath had to be tied around my waist. I was a city-dweller, a farmer, a carpenter, a butcher. I lived and worked both in and outside the city. I was a house-builder, a weaver, I spun and dyed wool. I was a soldier, held a spear; I was a merchant with my money-bag under my tunic.

When the blast of the trumpets announced the game, the man in the mirror resembled the one in the picture I was holding; and I looked exactly like the men depicted in the museum painting.

The young attendant came again to escort me. When I arrived in the arena, all the players were already standing in their circles. I was shown my place. I was a pawn, on the very spot where I had stood three days ago.

The trumpets fell silent. In the opening speech, the mayor thanked the guests, stressing the importance of the game for his town.

The bleachers were completely full but the spectators were perfectly silent.

Once the players were in their places on the field, they must remain motionless, since they were "the pieces" in the mayor's game; the mayor particularly stressed this requirement. For this reason, I couldn't move my head or look around.

    The mayor stood to our right, on the platform specially built for him. He sat in his chair. After another round of trumpets, the game began.

"KILL ME, MASTER!"

. . . As it turns out, some very old mothers and fathers, once turned into demons, attempt to eat humans, even their own children at times. As for the mother in our tale, her children performed her funeral rites. In retrospect, it was a horrifying affair. That's how people remember it being described.

from "A Mother of Hunters"
(12th-century Japanese folktale)

Children have to outlive their mother to take care of her funeral. Yet, the opposite is known to have happened as well.

Flying from trapeze to trapeze, from tightrope to tightrope, acrobats sometimes fall and die. Death knows no age, and there is the young acrobat who says: "As soon as I see a mole growing just below an acrobat's right nostril—a mole that only I can see—I know it means he will die, like all the others; but whether he falls off the tightrope, or a car hits him, or he doesn't survive an illness, that part I can never tell . . ."

You approach each other from the two ends of the tightrope, and act as if you're wrestling; then one of you pretends to lose and fall while the other leaps after him, catches him in the air and saves his life; you strike panic in everybody's heart, then the two of you swing and grab another tightrope, another trapeze, and that's how you earn your daily bread.

The acrobat facing you is someone you love, someone

you have worked with for years, someone who has shared your unrelenting pains as well as those rare moments of joy that still manage to visit you when you have accustomed yourself to saying, "We never smile." Let's say he is someone like that. You approach the middle of the tightrope, face to face. All of a sudden, below his right nostril— Then the rush of questions . . . What are you—a young acrobat—supposed to do . . .

Let's start over.

The one facing him was his master.

In a sense, isn't the master also supposed to have mastered the way to stay alive?

His master, the one facing him, the one who had taken him in as a young boy, who had raised him, taught him the art, brought him all the way here and made him the most famous of young acrobats.

For a long time, theirs had been much more than a master-apprentice relationship. The young one perceived himself as his master's "son," who in turn also treated him as his son, and introduced him to others as "my son." Yet the master didn't want to be seen as just any master calling an apprentice his "son"; he took pains not to address him as "my son" directly, not even to speak his name when he wanted to tell him something. In any case, their conversation always started at mid-sentence, continuing from where it had left off a day or a week ago; or they brought it to a conclusion as if they had already recounted its beginning. If one ever let a sound escape his throat to draw the other's attention, both men felt ashamed, coughed and cleared their throats, trying to wipe out, to obliterate that sound from the air it had seeped into. For them, an absentminded moment, the slightest pause of uncertainty as to where the talk had been left off or where it was supposed to go, a raised eyebrow, a twitch of the eye or the lip, was at least as shameful as calling each other by name.

Because of this, their friends and peers often found it difficult to follow their conversation, and cast puzzled glances
at them. So familiar with their private habits, the two
couldn't fathom that there were people in the world who
found their way of talking strange. They attempted to talk
in the same manner with others, but seeing the raised eyebrows, the unashamed twitching of eyes or lips, they soon
gathered themselves, and—as if startled out of a slumber,
as if awakened but drowsy—they floundered awkwardly,
breaking into a sweat, struggling to make comprehensible
conversation.

True, the young one perceived himself as the older
man's son; yet, he saw his master not as a father—rather as
a mother—one who gave him birth, nursed and raised
him, and taught him how to live. Early on, the odd nature of the feeling frightened him, made him uneasy, and
he thought that he could not reveal something as outlandish as this even to his master who was privy to his every
thought. Eventually, he came to realize that his reticence
was even stranger than his feeling (no matter how odd that
was), and one night after the performance, while the two
were lying in the dark, he let out what was inside him. At
first, restrained chuckles came from the bed in the opposite corner. What a mistake he'd made, saying such a
thing, even to his master! Yet, as he was about to crawl
through the rubble of the world that had collapsed on
him, his master's chuckles turned into loud, steady laughter. And only just before daybreak did the peals of laughter
subside; that's when the master said, "What a poet's soul
you have!" and started snoring. His outlandish idea had
made his master laugh; yet, obviously it had pleased him,
too. The world which had collapsed on his head gathered
itself back, order was restored. And never again was this
feeling mentioned, which was characteristic of their
union, their companionship.

Many months later, however, as he feigned a misstep

and let himself fall toward the trapeze swinging beneath them, the hands of his master who caught and "rescued" him in the air reminded him of something. After the performance, he collected his pay from the boss, bid everyone goodnight, got dressed, and walked home alongside his master, and all along he kept trying to figure out that vague reminiscence, what it was, what it meant. He couldn't. The next evening, as he was again "falling" toward the trapeze—

In the confusion of his mind, he recognized: The motherly quality he found in his master had nothing to do with poetry or literature. He remembered a childhood episode: day after day standing in front of a closed door, listening to the moans coming from his uncle's room. They would not let him into the room. Because they would not let him in—and, as a rule, he avoided certain rooms of the house unless he was pushed through the door—he had spent many a night quietly sitting on the doorstep of their house. So on that particular day, he stood in front of the door, listening to the moans, but this time he was gently pushing the door. Nobody was around. That is, his mother wasn't, his grandmother—

As the trapeze drew close, his master's hands that were supposed to grab him by his waist, barely caught him by his wrists.

They were his mother's hands!

That night, when they were back in their room, his master began to chastise him, and more severely than he had ever before. Yet, after the endless tirade, the master asked, "Tell me, why did it happen, how could you have lost focus?" and the young man realized that he wasn't listening, that he was pretending to listen, that he thought he was listening—

He told his master everything, from start to finish. As if he were seeing it, living it right there and then. Starting with the details the master already knew: His father had

died, his grandmother had become senile, his uncle was
bringing in the income, and his mother was taking care of
the house and everybody living in it. At the time, it must
have been just two or three months since his second birthday, because his mother had told him so afterwards. Besides, he could still picture himself—as if looking in the
mirror—while remembering all this. He was dressed in a
loose robe made of cloth printed with red and green flowers. His grandmother sat in her strange, low armchair
with supports on all sides. She never left her armchair.
Underneath it, there was a chamber pot that his mother
emptied when the smell became strong; this chamber pot
was rounder, larger, and brighter red than his. Because of
the warmer weather, he had been spending his days sitting
on the porch, from morning till sunset. That morning, his
mother had moved his grandmother and her armchair out
on the porch and set her in front of the door. His grandmother always dozed off. His mother wasn't around. She
had left in a hurry, telling him that she would be back
right away. He was too small to reach the round, shiny
doorknob. But on that day when he leaned against the
door, he found it slowly yielding to his weight, and in
the end, he managed to squeeze through and enter the
house. As he walked, the moaning grew louder (the drapes
must have been drawn shut, it was dark as twilight inside,
he could still picture it); he approached his uncle, who was
lying on his stomach, and looked. Had his uncle noticed
him, had his lips tightened as if straining to smile or say
something, or had the gesture been an indication of his
lungs' last struggle? Even now he couldn't say. Suddenly a
hand grabbed his wrists, another his robe, and quietly ushered him outside: his mother's hands. As for the other
man—who must have come with his mother—he shook
his head when leaving the room. His mother squatted on
the doorstep and, without speaking, held her head between her hands. Frightened, he did not speak; then, he

extended his arm and touched his mother's knee. When his mother's hand moved down from her forehead and rested on his hand, his fear disappeared. He started thinking of what he had noticed on his uncle's face, just below the right nostril (he could still picture it; that's why he knew right from left), the big blot, the mole he had never seen before.

That night, after listening to all this, his master again chastised him. But only very briefly this time, even though the young pupil listened intently. You can't remember such things, his master told him, you can't remember them while working. One of these days, the hands that would save him from death might not find his waist or wrists.

If this was what his master wanted, then the young man could not hold on to his memories, to his past; from now on he would think of his work and nothing else, concentrate his mind on his master and no one else. He had to erase his memories from his consciousness, the memories of his mother's death, his grandmother's death; and he erased them.

He erased them, yes, but one memory defied all effort. He could not forget the moles that he had seen growing below the right nostrils of the two women whose faces he knew so well that he thought he could almost draw them from memory. The moles that became noticeable in the span of a few days, seizing him with sadness each time he saw one and wondered, "How could I have failed to notice it!" The moles that reached almost the size of an olive on the day of their death—

He realized. These moles must have been a family trait. They only appeared shortly before death, they grew, and on the final day became as large as—

He was still quite young. He had not yet learned to doubt knowledge gained without the necessary reflection, sifting and scrutiny. One day, while training his master's new apprentice on the tightrope—

It was a summer day. Only the acrobats knew the dread of working so near the roof of the tent on hot days. His master was watching from below, shouting directions. He wanted his new apprentice to climb the tightrope within a week and perform for the spectators. The young boy had to work hard. They couldn't expect their master to come all the way up in such heat, and besides, elevated to the rank of the assistant, it was his duty to train the new apprentice.

They stopped in the middle of the tightrope, facing each other. Now pay attention, he told the new boy standing in front of him, wipe your sweat well, we don't need any accidents . . . The boy wiped himself and said, "Ready," while looking into his eyes. Just then, the assistant saw the mole below the right nostril of the apprentice. They continued practice, and when it was over, they descended. While in the shower, he teased the young boy, saying, "That mole makes you handsome." At first the young boy gave him a funny look. Then he asked, "What mole are you talking about?" He looked in the mirror and could see nothing. In a slightly hurt voice, he said that he didn't get the joke. The assistant then replied, "It was probably a smudge, forgive me, I mistook it for a mole." But the next day when they resumed training, he again saw the mole in the same spot. And it was even more noticeable. Three days later when the young boy was training alone on the middle tightrope, he fell off and died. When the other one ran up to him, he saw that the mole was still there, as big as an olive . . .

This was not a family trait, then; it only belonged to him. He alone saw the moles, no one else did—

He knew that they would die. Time and again, the sign proved infallible. He began dreading looking people in the face.

Later on, he did not see any moles for some time. No one died around him. He felt a little relieved.

The willow trees belong to the same period.

One spring evening, he and his master were returning home. Only the two of them. The master and his son. All three of the apprentices who sought training alongside the master had died—he had seen the mole on all of them, but not all had died by falling off the tightrope—and after the third, no one else wanted to apprentice himself to the master. Some people reasoned that it wasn't the master's fault, that the boy must have the mark of the jealous brother. They came and looked, staring intently at the spot between his eyebrows, and some did see there the mark they expected to see while others saw nothing. One morning, even his master searched for the mark on his face. He couldn't see it. At least, so he said. Yet, later, in the soft glow of the morning light, one day the assistant noticed a mark between his master's eyebrows. Instead of the purple fork of the jealous brother, the greenish scalpel of the father who rejects his sons. He did not tell this to his master, he could not tell him. And anything he could not tell his master would not stay in his mind. And it didn't. He forgot it completely.

They were both feeling sad about these developments; but eventually they also grew accustomed to not having to share their way of life with others.

That spring evening, they walked alongside the willow garden on their way home, and saw that all the trees had been pruned; only that morning they'd enjoyed noticing the dew-like shimmer of the sprightly, delicate leaves on the very branches now piled on the sidewalk. His master stepped down onto the street in order to avoid treading on the branches, but the young boy walked over the piles, stepping on the branches gently, respectfully, lovingly, with the utmost agility of his acrobat's feet. Afterwards, he stopped and, smelling the air for a long, long time, he tried to explain to his master how he yearned to be near the water, surrounded by the green, the grass, the cattails.

His master chastised him again. Did he not know well that an acrobat worked and earned a living in densely populated places? And generally speaking, densely populated places had no streams or rivers with willow and cattails. If they did, fine, but such yearnings were not for an acrobat who knew himself, especially one who spent most of his time in big cities. The acrobat had to think of his tightrope; yearnings, dreams, these he had to erase from his heart.

If his master said so, he would erase them. And he did so. After the memories, he also erased the yearnings from his heart. What mattered was his master; his whole upbringing had been a tutorial on the importance of his work. His master had taught him this—his work was his identity. Nothing else. This dedication to work, he owed to his master. Didn't his master mother him? Didn't he learn everything from him? Yet could it be *everything*? Did he not shape his own identity, at least in part? Which parts of his identity did his master shape? Which parts did he shape on his own? And what did it mean to shape, really? Was he nothing when he first appeared in front of his master? Had he shaped him entirely? Then, was everyone shaped in the manner his master shaped him, or, no, in the manner that the master shaped himself in the apprentice . . .

He was confused. If he were to ask these questions of his master, he felt he knew the answers he would receive. His master wouldn't say, "You're not ready to grasp these questions." But he thought so himself. "I am not ready to grasp them now," he said, "but will there come a day when I will be ready?" No, his master wouldn't say any of this. Instead he would just say, "Don't think!" The master would say, "After I die hire an apprentice and begin to train him, then you can start thinking about these matters and come to understand both yourself and me." The young man felt like he had already heard these words.

Which meant that at least a part of him could rise to the level of, and perhaps even exceed, his master's intelligence. He was able to think these thoughts by himself . . . But he didn't fret over this any more. The acrobat's art—if one didn't want to die—required full concentration on the tightrope, the trapeze, the master, the steps, the hands and eyes. If one day he met someone who was not an acrobat but a thinker, he would ask him these questions. Of course, whether or not that person had given any thought to an acrobat's questions was another matter . . .

While doing somersaults on the tightrope and being watched by the undulant sea of spectators below, he noticed that from time to time his mind was still distracted by questions instead of focusing on the tightrope. This was unacceptable. He couldn't let his master notice his lapses. He resolved to purge his mind of all questions. He stopped thinking while at work. Yet during their long travels from city to city, he would pretend to sleep—even fooling his master—and lose himself among the willows of questions, the damp cattails of questions.

Before each performance, they distributed leaflets, slipped them under the doors in the neighborhood, dropped them at the cafés and card-parlors, and handed them out on the streets. Each night when they returned home, his master carefully placed a copy of the leaflets inside his special trunk. But one night his master turned to him and said, "You're ready, you have become a master acrobat, I am leaving this task to you." The young man shunned the heart-pleasing effect of the words, and ventured to ask instead, "Aren't these also memories, Master?" That's when his master went into a rage. "So you are not ready yet! These are not memories," he scolded him, "they are the only signs we will have left behind; they are our way of life, the inventory of our experiences, the sum total of our lives. With each passing day the weight of death creeps on to our shoulders, with each performance, and it will finally crush us on the day when we can no longer carry this trunk, mark my words! These leaflets are you and me. What else do we have to prove, whether to ourselves or to others, that we have lived, what else besides this pile of papers?"

And that night, after being scolded like this, everything became clear. Not because of the leaflets but because of his master's rage. How could he not have sensed it until that night?

These eruptions of rage, these assaults meant to verbally crush him—or more precisely, his youth—went beyond the normal anger of a master-apprentice relationship.

He should have noticed long time ago that these outbursts were different.

My master has aged. Have I been too preoccupied with growing older and mastering my art that I had no time to notice that others are also growing, aging? Living with him all the time, have I lost the habit of looking at his face? The young man got angry at his own blindness. In truth, we want our loved ones to grow with our love but we don't want them to age and approach death. Since I've come to recognize this odd contradiction, it must mean I have aged too. As for him, who know how close he is to the end? The young man followed the train of his thoughts this far but resisted thinking further. Or he couldn't.

His master had aged. Previously, he had thought that his master's reproaches were directed at him, but now he understood that between these recent outbursts and the old reproaches of his childhood, his novice years, there was . . .

How could he have slept through all this? So long as he thought that his master could do nothing wrong, that he could say nothing wrong. . . .

Yet nowadays, never mind pointing out any mistakes,

god help him if he mentioned something that could be construed as suggesting that his master might have overlooked something, even something very small! Without fail, the angry outbursts followed. And it served him right. Didn't he dare to think and, worse yet, hint at thoughts he had never let visit his mind before? Of course his master had every right to be angry.

With each passing day the young man became more and more aware of his thoughts, and what used to be intuitions soon gave way to the conviction that he wasn't mistaken. He was a master of his own thoughts now. Yet, so much so that he could keep them at bay while he was performing.

If a master builder spends an entire lifetime building an edifice, carrying its stones one by one, raising its walls with his own hands, and if, near the end of his work, he is shown a crack, a gap, an error discovered in one of the walls, his anger . . .

Or was the young man beginning to feel a little too self-important and therefore noticing his master's shortcomings? Or could it be that the shadows and intimations of failure were making his master all the more anxious, all the more prone to fail? Wasn't his master a human being, like everybody else? Like everybody else, didn't he have to go through old age, a season of decline? What set his master apart besides that he was a "master"—the only quality that made him superior to those who were otherwise his equals? The apprentice couldn't be certain but knew that certainty would help very little. Since the earliest days, his master seldom, if ever, showed any restraint in embarrassing his beloved apprentice, his beloved novice, by pointing out his deficiencies in public. Yet when the young man had one day mentioned the trunk full of leaflets in front of others, he had been treated to a fine scolding by his master. All this vexed and confused him. He wasn't supposed to talk about the things his master didn't want others to know about, but now his master was merrily divulging certain things, giving little thought to whether the apprentice was pleased or displeased by the public disclosures. He didn't mean to annoy the apprentice, he wasn't being a pig—clearly, that wasn't the case. He simply couldn't imagine that anything in his stories could harm or upset his beloved apprentice. The master was, after all, incapable of imagining that he could make mistakes.

In the end the young man decided. No matter what, he would not get angry with his master or forget that he had gotten old, and even when he noticed his master's mistakes, he would keep his mouth shut so as not to hurt him. Two days ago, while they were drinking their morning tea, his master had suddenly started talking: "I dread the day when I will need help to live. The day when I will need your help to live . . . From time to time I tell myself, I should have no help so I can die like a dog . . . But I am not sure which is worse: the pain of being a burden or the pain of loneliness. . . ." He could still hear his master's words and they had obviously played a part in his decision. But the night when he made his decision, he felt relieved, he slept a seamless sleep, of the kind he had not enjoyed in a long time.

The next morning they were again sitting together and drinking their morning tea; all of a sudden he noticed a dark spot just below his master's right nostril. He almost reached out to wipe it off, but held back. His master knew the meaning of the moles, and would have been distressed. The young man couldn't even bear the thought.

That day the city was mourning an eminent person's death. There would be no performance in the evening. He decided to walk to the countryside. Soon he found a frail little creek, a paltry outcropping of willow trees. He lay down and gazed at the sky, letting his mind wander . . . The terror of his master's death seized his heart. Suppose he was wrong and his master would not die soon. Still,

wasn't the thought unleashing terror in his heart for the
first time? It meant that he could imagine his master's
death. He could now think about it. In a way, he could feel
happy, too. He would become the master, take apprentices, train them, he would be able to think, seek answers
to the myriad questions he had gathered over the years,
he would be able to seek, try to find answers. But he,
too—

He remembered the apprentices who had died. Was it
because of their deaths that his master had grown so attached to him? I had three different apprentices before
you, he had said one day, all three had accidents; after you
arrived, I didn't want anybody else, I had to put all my energy into training you, and if I am hiring this new boy
now, it's because you have come so far. . . . (The master
was referring to the boy whom the young man had trained
on the tightrope, the same one below whose right nostril
he had seen the mole. It was the evening of the day when
they had taken the boy in. The master had said all this
after putting the boy to bed, when the two had sat outside
the door. In the rumbling heat of the summer night.) After
that boy, two more apprentices had died.

Wasn't his master like those mothers whose children
were stillborn? Or who had miscarriages? The young man
had reached the assistant's rank, and was very close to becoming a master. What if he were to die also? His master
would wither and die of remorse, because his assistant had
died as a youth on the verge of mastery. Then he would
have failed to train anyone. . . . Some masters were
considered unlucky among the acrobats because their
protégés—apprentices, assistants—died always in their
youth. . . . Clearly his master was like them. Of course,
no poor soul would dare to speak of anything like this to
his face or when he was around. Yet, spoken or not, was it
not still the case? The art, the acrobat's art, was evidently
languishing on account of such masters. Like people dying

without progeny. Granted, many masters rose to distinction and quite a few came close to attaining true greatness. But those withering branches, weren't they like barren women? One master or another had raised each of them. Yet they, in turn, would raise none. In other words, they were not the ones withering; the ones withering were the saplings meant to grow out of them.

Yet, he was still living. He took out his hand-mirror and examined his face. There wasn't even a speck of dust, much less a mole. It meant that he would live, that his master would have raised an heir and escaped the ill-fated legacy. That his master had to die in order to escape, that his apprentice, now his assistant—who would attain the master's rank after his master's death—had to live, in a sense.

He didn't like the direction his thoughts had taken, and found the strange convergence of the ridiculous and the serious—of comedy and tragedy—utterly confusing.

He slept then woke up. The sun was slipping westward. Almost time to return to the cage, he said unexpectedly. He surprised himself. Where did the thought come from? Since when . . .

That morning his master had put the teacup on the table and walked to the mirror. Could he also see the mole below his right nostril? Like a cruel hand, the question reached in and wrenched the young man's heart; then he said to himself, He may be the master, but it's unlikely that he can see the mole. Only the young man saw the moles. He had no reason to think that his master could see them. In any case, the old man had checked his eyes and eyebrows more than his nose. So it had seemed. Then the master had turned around and said, "We're not practicing today; you don't have to walk the tightrope either. No sense in spending your day with old men. We're at death's door, anyway." Either he had seen the mole—but that was impossible—or these words were just an eerie coincidence. The young man had felt a knot in his throat. Only later, he had somehow managed to protest, "Don't talk like this. You have not taught me how to respond to such words, I don't know what to say." His master had smiled and said, "Hurry up and go outside."

The cage. It existed. Both his words and those of his master served as ample proof.

The cage signaled escape. And escape signaled—

Didn't he want to become a great acrobat? Hadn't he toiled all these years to become a master? Madly loved his work, his art, his life of the acrobat—

What did it mean to love something madly? The question hadn't occurred to him until that day. Does one love the air? One breathes the air in and lives. That's all. This, too, was an expression, a cliché, something he had always heard, and one day, used to his advantage.

He loved his work more than madly. He would never abandon his work. There was nothing without it. But he loved his master, too. He could never abandon him either.

Still, whose hand, if not his master's hand, was responsible for all these obsessions, these passions? Whether obsession or love, it didn't matter. He would return to the cage.

In the evening, he looked at his master's face; the mark under his nose seemed to have grown a little larger. He was filled with countless anxieties. They overwhelmed all the thoughts he had experienced when he was by the creek. On the third day, he had no doubt. His master would die. The mole was growing.

He lost his mind. He didn't know what to do; feeling utterly helpless, he watched the mole growing on his master's face. In the last few days, they had resumed performing the perilous wrestling routine that they had discontinued some time ago. He had his heart in his mouth while wrestling on the tightrope, terrified that he would cause his master's death, and he was all the more distraught that his feeling of panic would hasten the accident. He knew that his death would be like no other, that, all of the sudden, he would plunge into a terrible loneliness; and the more he imagined, the more he wanted to beat his head against the walls. That would be a better end, he thought

some would think so

some would not be afraid to think so, he had a vague feeling, there ought to be people who would not be afraid, yet

It was maddening to watch the mole grow bigger each day, and he felt exasperated by the need to hide the fact from his master, the only man in the world he could confide in.

The evening when the mole was as big as an olive, he balanced his tense body on the tightrope and watched his master approach him. He arrived. They held each other. It was his master's turn to perform the pretend false-step. He was arched as a bow, ready to leap after his master and catch him in the air. Since he never again wanted to anger his master, who erupted and raged with fears that the walls he had kept building for years could be toppled by the slightest flick of the finger, the young man would not point out after the performance that his master had been late in taking the false step, he would not even let the other sense that he had noticed the delay. Let the morning come, he thought, I'll figure out something, maybe I'll tell him I'm not feeling well, who knows, maybe I'll suggest that we cancel practice, or that it is too hot for him to go up on the tightrope, or I can offer to entertain the spectators as much as I can by myself . . . Ideas stormed through his mind but he was pretty certain that none would fool his master, and this made him anxious. Determined to appear calm, he loosened his muscles, ready to counteract his master's every move. Never mind if the spectators would notice, for the first time he was determined to prove—first to himself, then to his master—that he had become a masterful acrobat. So what if the master was a master, *his* master! He still had to notice the transformation, he had no choice but to kiss him on the forehead and declare that the young man was now a master. This was the moment of proof. Perhaps his master was testing him, unaware of the fear inside his assistant's heart, thinking that his protégé was unaware of the test. Because, after all the apprentices he had lost, the master wanted to feel proud that this one attained mastery, because he wanted the satisfaction of having witnessed this day before he died, before he was defeated altogether. But didn't these thoughts prove otherwise—that the young man had not yet earned the master's status? Even as his master was fading away before his very eyes . . .

He was waiting. Still waiting for his master to take the last step.

Yet his master had already grabbed the trapeze below the middle tightrope. As the young man flashed toward the sand-covered stage encircled by spectators, he failed to discern among the shouts, the screams, his master's voice saying, "Alas, my careless son!" He couldn't hear.

1970

8.

*A*t first, only small groups of nomads appeared in the forests surrounding the territories. Leaving behind their cold prairies, their glaciers, their swamplands, to fight hunger they came down south, raiding towns, farms and markets. When they first appeared their cattle looked as starved as themselves. The hunting grounds and the pastures up north no longer sustained them. They were tired of eating horses, dogs. In their winter settlements, they no longer wished to eat root vegetables.

They increased in numbers. They laid siege to the territories of the wealthy overlord. When the time was right, they attacked from four directions, pillaged the land, and retreated.

Only on the fourth raid were they able to reach the overlord's heavily guarded castle. At each raid, the surviving peasants would seek shelter in the castle. The overlord was aware of the growing number of his soldiers who were ripe for vengeance and eager to fight for the land, but he was waiting for the right *time. The battlefield had to be narrow to give them a fighting chance against the swarming forest nomads.*

But they failed, though they fought and died valiantly.

The overlord had to endure ceaseless waves of pillaging, the destruction of his land, his roads, his houses and subjects. At last, he conceded and migrated south.

Two or three hundred years later, the overlord witnessed once again the onslaught of the plunderers who again came from the forests. Into the new territories.

• • •

The nomads were no longer living in transient winter settlements, wearing robes of wool and animal fur, or sleeping on horseback. The nomad was no longer in search of water; he had grown to enjoy the taste of clean, abundant water. What he now wanted was not a brook or a spring; he was after the fountains, the baths, the river, the sea.

The overlord in the new territories possessed all of that.

But this time, he sought for a way to avoid defeat, and found it. He reached an agreement with the enemy: the game was born.

• • •

The mayor took his seat after calling for the game to begin. But before the first move, the shadow of the palace had to reach and cover the ornate fountain. We waited. His tall body rose behind the green pawns lined up in front of me. Under the noon sun, his hair had a golden-brown glow. He was looking at me. How could I, a lowly pawn . . .

(Besides, we, the Purple team, were under the mayor's control. He would determine every one of our moves, and we would simply obey, whereas the Greens were on their own. They were free to determine among themselves the best move and make it. All of them were foreigners.

Ten of the Purples were natives; six were chosen among the foreigners to represent the provinces, but we, too, had to obey the mayor.)

. . . defeat a Vizier like him?

Without a game-master guiding the Greens, it was more difficult for them to decide on the right moves. Yet, I was no more than a subservient pawn.

The shadow reached the fountain. The mayor gave his first order and moved me forward.

OVR SEA

To the AcromaSea . . .

The children were playing on the stretch of the shore where the sand could be kneaded like wet clay. The waves, chasing one another as if gliding over the warm, soft backs of furry animals, reached the children's feet, their hands, and then died out, vanishing in the sand. Wet sand caked their buttocks, forming little circles. Not yet sure what to build, the children kneaded the wet sand into balls, packed them in moulds, moved them a little further away, then crumbled them up and kneaded them anew. They dug holes, knelt before each, piled the sand they scooped out on one side, stomping and packing it with the soles of their feet. They tossed into the holes the cigarette butts they found, and the sticks and twigs, and the large pebbles with sea-glazed surfaces. They'd bury all that by pushing the sand back into the holes, and then dig new ones. They were quiet. Everything amused them. From time to time, they seemed about to quarrel over a pebble they couldn't share, a piece of driftwood, a little twig, but then they quickly buried it in the wet sand, removing from sight anything that would rouse discord. Pebbles and—if one knew where to look—driftwood were both plentiful along the shore. At one point, the torn corner of an envelope carried by the breeze brushed against their feet, which made them a little uneasy. Its stamp was still bright with glossy colors, unmarred. One of them managed to remove the stamp without tearing or creasing it; the others kept watching him, their mouths wide open, their pupils large with excitement; the boy paused, then pasted the stamp on to his chest and raised his fist; all the outstretched hands remained suspended in the air. Then, the stamp, too, joined the objects buried in the hole. They quietly carried on with their games.

> Behind them, very far behind them, under the brush, a lizard was startled by the silence; with a slight rustle, it swished and disappeared.

The women sat under the tent, not very far from the children. They talked, leaned back, dozed off, and then, waking up, resumed their conversation. Two boys sat away from them, at the opposite corner of the tent. Burnt in the sun, their already swarthy, southern skins had turned even darker. They dipped in the sea just to cool off a little, and quickly returned to the tent. They were doing homework, perhaps preparing for exams. Every now and then, their voices would grow slightly loud, and a serious-minded scientific term or a bookish word or two would flutter in the air—sweating even under the tent—and over the sand, scattering right and left.

> From the brush behind the sandy shore came a lizard, which climbed on a large rock. Its belly pulsating on the rock that had soaked up the sun's blistering heat.

Two men were in the sea. They swam, each moment ad-
miring anew the sea's myriad shades of green, the deep
tadpole green, the peacock-plume green, the translucent
jellyfish green, the fresh-plum green. They weren't in the
sea just to cool themselves or to really swim. Rather, to be
in the water, to experience the joy of making whole the
half-freedom of their arms, their legs, their bodies, to spin
in the ever-yielding water, to feel—almost—the salt mixing with their blood . . . This salt-water conundrum always excited both men, their thoughts lazing about inside
their minds: a believe-it-or-not kind of title noticed many
years ago, and below the title, a methodical exposition on
the similarity between human blood and sea water. This
comparison's concepts of salts, water, medium, were easy
to follow, but when it came to color, fluidity, temperature,
the two men would pause and laugh at the presumption of
sameness. Fine, we lower the temperature, they would say,
we increase the fluidity so that blood won't clot, dry out
and drop off in clumps. We'd still need to find a way to
transform the color . . . They would laugh at the comparison. Come on, let's try harder, they would say, let's be
more intelligent; to transform the color . . . They would
laugh and say that the challenge demanded not more intelligence, rather, less. Yet, a certain degree of intelligence
was still needed in order to lessen one's dependence on intelligence, and this fact—solid and unyielding—came
pressing against their faces, in the perfect stillness of the
deep sea. A way to transform the color . . .

> At one end of the sandy shore, in a muddy
> stretch of the streambed where the water had
> much receded, a frog croaked, frightened, as if
> sensing a threat. It leapt toward the pebbles
> heaped between the sea and the stream. Chang-
> ing its mind, it took three leaps and ran toward

> the upper bed. Where it sensed it could still find
> a deep green puddle . . .

The men were gazing at the shore. The breeze was so
light that it couldn't even carry the salt of the sea; it only
deposited dust and sand in the nostrils, the ears, the belly
buttons of those sitting under the tent . . . The children
had one foot in the dust, the other in the sand. For now,
the salt entirely belonged to those in the sea. The water
belonged to them, and the light wind now and then lick-
ing and creasing the water belonged to them. Only the
sun sided with those on the shore. But the two men were
laughing, telling themselves, we still have fire, fire is still
inside us. And now they're thinking that they could use
this knowledge to their advantage, against the sea of the
same nature as human blood. They wouldn't reduce the
temperature yet. True, the color still remained beyond
their grasp. To reduce the red of fire, to reduce it to the
green of plums, leaves, seaweed, peppers. . . . The pepper's fire was green, for instance . . . Aha! Perhaps they
were on the right track. Reduced. . . . It had to be reduced. It was worth trying.

> Breathing on the blistering rock behind the
> sandy shore, the lizard was startled by a noise in-
> side the brush; it jumped, then dived. Hid un-
> derneath the rock. The greenish silvery color of
> its skin matched the sand in the cool shade.
> Through the parting stems came a weary cat,
> who sniffed the surface of the rock, the bottom,
> looked around and, finding nothing, gave up
> looking and walked away.

The tall one said, "My feet are touching the bottom." A
little farther away, the medium-built one replied, "And
I can kneel now." Their heads were above the water,
unmoving. "We're nearing the shore. That's it," said

the tall one. "Whooeee!" agreed the other. "Whooeee! Whooeee!" echoed the tall one. They laughed. This was a sound of approval in the language of a faraway country, learned from the movies. "But we can't come out just yet," said the tall one. "Our heads are above the water, we know we won't drown, but we still don't know our enemies . . . Are they around? Who are they?" They could barely suppress their laughter. The medium-built one said, "Let's stay in the water, crawl on our hands and knees, and when we reach the shallow water, let's slither on our bellies; let's not come out until we've surveyed the shore carefully, Whooeee?" "Whooeee," said the tall one. But they were no longer laughing; now they were ancient many-finned creatures from a distant sea, stealthily approaching the shore. Slowly, slowly. They were trying to feel—to experience—the circumspection of that first primordial creature to crawl out on to the shore. Soon their backs felt the sun's warmth, their skin began to burn. They felt more and more the chafing rasp of the sand on their chests; pebbles rolled under their bellies. Afraid, hesitant, they extended their hands simultaneously, toward the sand that was still wet yet no longer sheltered by the sea. Both the tall man and the medium-built man calmly observed four front fins stabbing into the sand. Just above the fins now covered with damp sand, above the claws, wet scales glistened with a silvery greenish hue. Cautiously, reluctantly, they distended their bellies. They raised their heads. Little by little, with much difficulty, they turned them to the right, then to the left. On the shore, immense blotches of color emitted sharp, piercing sounds. Slowly turning their heads to face each other, they saw large orbs—their icy, bare, inert, protuberant eyes. Crawling, crawling, they moved ashore. An exposed nail on a piece of wood in their path left a long white scratch across the thigh of the tall one. A little later, the other one noticed a few drops of blood seeping through the now-rosy whiteness, and he wanted to say, "Look, our blood is still red," gazing at his companion. "It hurts!" the tall one wanted to say. The two eyed each other, motionless; they stared for a long long time. Their mouths opened. Not a grunt came out, much less a voice. It couldn't.

1969

9.

*E*ach time the Greens won the game, they would live for ten years in the palace and the houses in town. When the Purples won, the Greens would retreat to the forest for ten years and live on provisions sent by the townspeople.

Soon, they became friends. The game came to be played for the sake of tradition. Who knows how many of the Purple players had ancestors among the forest people.

• • •

We were "stone" game pieces, and after each time we were moved we froze like stones. My gaze was fixed on him.

I knew that he, too, was thinking of me, watching me and no one else. The Greens constantly weighed their moves and communicated with their eyes. They were restless, barely able to stay put. The animal pendants on their chains—the little silver horses, dogs, roe deer—kept swinging about, as the players swung around themselves and communicated without words.

Their pawns were carrying spears, horseshoes, axes and lassoes. By now we were quite spread out on the field.

I was in danger a few times. I kept in mind the hotel attendant's words, "Do whatever you can to be captured," but nothing was up to me. Besides I didn't like the idea of captivity. My goal was to capture him. The Greens were very skilled, obviously. The mayor was taking longer and longer to decide each move, and as the sun moved westward, we were feeling the fatigue of being so still. I don't know how many moves later, I finally had the sun behind me. Not to see him, not being able to look at him cast a darkness about me.

With obvious mastery, the mayor defended himself, his waters, houses and palace, while I was unable to satisfy my one yearning: to see him.

From the bleachers I felt eyes, hundreds of them, watching me, even though I knew they didn't need to. They forgot that the players were human beings. The game was all that mattered since we, too, were expected

to forget that we were human . . .

A giant poplar tree stood between the towering bleachers crammed with people. Suddenly emerging from behind the tree, two green eyes fixed themselves at me. Moving slowly, the small form crossed the playing field and came toward me. It was a scrawny alley cat, its ears and muzzle scarred from street fights. Approaching me, it sniffed my feet and rubbed itself against them. Some of the spectators noticed the cat and laughed. But silence was soon restored. It was our turn. The mayor was thinking.

Finally, he called on me. As I made my move, we came face to face. For the first time he seemed to be smiling. I smiled back.

HVRT ME NOT

To Tözün and Fred

This is the tale of a man who longed to be naked in a world where all people—we should probably say, "most people"—live and toil to clothe themselves; if not to weigh down their backs with clothes, then to keep warm in the bitter cold of winter.

• • •

He came here naked, thinking that the people on this warm island would not find his nakedness odd or subject him to insufferable questions. Yes, the island had its share of winter and the occasional harsh winds from the open sea. When absolutely necessary he would wear a sweater, after all. He wanted to own nothing else, although, quite strangely and in spite of himself, his wealth continued to increase.

He neither traded nor stole, nor did he try to flatter his neighbors on the hill in order to get free meals or heating.

The hill's residents were the grandchildren of

those who had, after the great earthquake centuries ago, moved their dwellings up, away from the shore, fearing the island would sink; the descendants of the oldest settlers, they fostered a tradition of giving, generously opening their homes, tables and coffers to others.

He lived by the water, in the part of town closest to the schools. He worked for all the schools, teaching various subjects. After all, teaching as many disciplines as he could and giving away his knowledge was also part of becoming naked.

By becoming naked, one achieves bare skin, pride, self-respect. Although these too are difficult to cast off, a person committed to the task of becoming naked knows when to take that last inevitable step, and die. All the same, he wants to take this final step among those who understand its value. When one mistakenly believes it is time and attempts the last act in unworthy company, it is a sad, sad story.

In addition to teaching, he was also asked to help with official correspondence because of his eloquence and penmanship.

There was plenty of correspondence. Everything from drinking water to flour was imported. The islanders exported fish. The people on the hill worked together with their neighbors on the shore. Bread was still baked in ovens by the sea and sent up the hills. The people on the hill believed that their forefathers had displayed acute wisdom by relocating after the earthquake. The island's order was nearly perfect. People diligently nursed their terror of earthquakes and made it their duty to pass that fear on to later generations. In the earthquake, the shores had crumbled and sunk. Most of the islanders had perished, their homes were destroyed and swept away. The survivors had moved their dwellings up the hills, and the inland shops spared by the earthquake had managed to continue their business. In later years, newcomers to the island were permitted to settle only by the sea; much later, families which had lived on the island for a few generations would be allowed to relocate to the hills.

In his native land, people had never known earthquakes, or, if they ever had, they'd long forgotten them. They worked the dependable soil to generate the best harvest, to reap the most robust seed from each seed sown. The rivers ran and the rains fell as abundantly as expected. Where necessary, giant transparent domes were built— over cities, over entire regions—to insure a mild, sustainable ecosystem for humans, animals and vegetation.

As the vegetation grew, so did the insects. The people fought against them but could not exterminate them altogether. Although the insects became fewer in number, they grew larger in size.

He dropped the water glass. He dropped the glass he took from the table. A significant event for the man who wanted to strip himself naked: it was unlike him to break or tear something deliberately. In the past, he'd reprimanded himself and grieved for hours over a broken glass or an accidentally torn shirt. Not because of the loss, not even if it was significant, but because of his own absentmindedness. That he could be so careless. Yet, today, he picked up the glass from the breakfast table, held it for a moment four feet above the stone tiles, then let go; and the shattering of glass sounded as familiar to him as the sea's steady surging, as pleasant as the waves breaking against rocks. That he'd cherished this glass, that it was a precious memento from a faraway land famous for its glassworks that he'd chosen after seeing it take shape in the hands of a master craftsman—none of that even crossed his mind.

Other animals also grew bigger. There were fewer of them, but those kept consuming in larger quantities. The harder the people worked to reap the robust seed, the more they resented the overgrown rats and insects stealing their food. Then began the migrations: People from faraway mountain villages started to move down, having heard fantastic stories for years about the wealth and grandeur of the valleys and cities. Not that they cared to claim a share of the wealth. It wasn't their style, coveting what they knew couldn't exist. When asked, they said, we came to see your elephant rats, your human-size ants. Although they soon realized that they'd been mistaken, few moved back to the mountains. Instead, they joined the fight to save the wheat fields from rats that were, after all, as big as dogs and ants as big as moles. They gradually got used to the life of the valleys, although they never quite overcame the shock of having left their mountain villages on account of fairy tales about giant beasts.

Year after year, people came up with new methods of protecting the seeds and the vegetation, at ever-increasing cost. Each attempt succeeded only briefly—the rats and insects always managed to survive, resuming their onslaught with an ever-greater appetite for destruction. People could not understand that the comfort they sought for themselves also suited other creatures and, since changing their way of living never occurred to them, they kept searching for new solutions to the problem. This constant courage was eclipsed by the abject futility of their solutions. At last, an inventive new generation came along and proposed new ways of living. Some of the new ideas proved successful but eventually led to even greater problems. As success lured people from villages to towns, from towns to cities, the huge snakes, rats and ants roamed freely around the fields and abandoned homes in the country, and when there was nothing left to gnaw on, these creatures, too, migrated to the cities—to find greater bounty, or death, perhaps.

At the time, he was about to graduate from one of the best schools in the largest domed region. One night at two a.m., returning home, he walked along rows of brightly lit stores. Tall garbage cans, filled to the brim, lined the sidewalk. A large mercurial dog with radiant coat stood on its hind legs, searching one of the bins, and tossing scraps of food to another dog—smaller but more beautiful— that was prancing around. He stopped and watched the dogs for some time. Suddenly, the small dog hopped off the sidewalk and was struck and dragged away by a fast-moving car. The large dog chased the car for a hundred and fifty feet, until the small dog could free itself. The car vanished from sight. The small dog's shrieks vanished into the darkness of the sidewalk on the other side of the street. He couldn't see the large dog anymore either. That night in his dreams, cars flew by, dragging humans and dogs, tossing them off at a distance. Mutilated, humans and dogs became indistinguishable, and the indifferent cars sped on in their terrifying, important race. The next day, he began to pack, and, three days later, he was on the road.

On the day he began teaching at one of the island schools, the small dog's howl was still in his ears.

He stood up without even thinking of picking up the shards, walked toward the door, glass crackling under his feet, and left for school. He was preoccupied. It took him a while to notice his students' agitation.

He never moved out of the first house he had settled into, one on the topmost row of houses by the sea, near the schools. The other teachers were natives of the island. Some lived by the sea, others on the hill. Because the schools were located between the hill and the coastal neighborhoods, they were out of danger. So he was told. He could live in one of the schools since he didn't own a house. . . . But he turned down the offer. He had heard that the residents of the hill took a lot of pride in their seniority, and that they didn't particularly enjoy becoming a minority, what with all the migrations to the island. But the distinction seemed forgotten—he hadn't witnessed any hillside-seaside rivalry. Those on the hill and those by the sea both sternly insisted that the newcomers observe the island's rules. But that was all.

For him, the earthquake carried no sense of reality. He noticed many newcomers easily absorbing the sense of imminent danger the island nursed so diligently, perhaps because they carried their own fear of past earthquakes with them. He was puzzled by this but tried not to show it.

Here is how matters stood on the island: If another earthquake struck and the shore were to crumble and vanish, some of those living by the sea would perhaps be spared, but the boatyards, the docks and bakeries would be destroyed; the people on the hill would save their homes and lives, but they would face hunger and abject poverty. As for those who lived by the sea, if they were to perish, they would prefer their bakeries and ships to perish along with them, and they refused to hear any of the occasional proposals to move the businesses uphill.

Along with the population of the island, businesses also multiplied and no one complained about unemploy-

ment or over-employment. The teacher's work also didn't
seem to increase or decrease. What he earned and how
much he could buy seemed to stay the same. Yet, perhaps
because he succeeded in remaining true to his principle of
casting everything off, his few modest needs must have
grown even fewer, since his wealth was actually increasing.
At first, he was intrigued; gradually he became anxious,
seized by fear.

His money was increasing faster and faster, it seemed.
He could not understand it. He thought of ways to deplete
his wealth, but all promised worse complications. If he
bought more and more, he would increase his possessions,
betraying his longing to be naked, and he would attract
more attention to himself. What was worse: to be perceived as a madman, or as someone who distrusted the stable order of the island, saving his money or attempting to
exchange it for durable goods? He was an outsider but not
like those who'd moved from nearby islands. Back where
he came from, people knew poverty, and they knew of
people who struck it rich but lost it all to start over from
pennies . . . Yet here, such twists of fate were terrifying.
He had been spared the stern rules with which the island
initially greeted the newcomers. Now to be perceived as
an outsider, and in the harshest manner imaginable, would
destroy the lifestyle that had taken him so long to build.
Had he really built a good way of life, or was he merely
imagining that he had? This question, too, started to pre-
occupy him lately.

> The end of May was near. Vacation would start
> soon. This morning, he opened the curtains that
> he kept closed to keep out the mosquitoes. A
> strange smell filled the room and his lungs. Like
> the smell of a garden, like the smell of railroad
> tracks, like the smell of an auto-repair shop.
> Smells that would not match or blend. Yet all

fused together into one smell. He thought of
gardens, railroad tracks, he thought of auto-
repair shops; a rush of images left over from different stages of his childhood swarmed before
his eyes. Then the images overlapped, drew together his distant childhood, the sea surrounding his present country, its smell, sounds, people, and became a single image embracing
everything. It was as though all the fragments of
his life had come together once again. This
wholeness lasted for perhaps two minutes as he
ardently inhaled the smell that came through
the window. When, overtaken by the joy of this
wholeness, he left the window to go to the
kitchen sink, he could not imagine that he must
let go of this emotion, and that this letting go
would be the most important step in becoming
naked. Long after he'd dropped the water glass,
he understood . . . On his way to school . . .
He suddenly realized the meaning of breaking
the glass. But it was too late. The feeling of all
his fragments coming together, the joy of having
become whole, was already a part of him. It
could not be uprooted. He had failed to let go at
the most crucial point. And the glass, he had
broken it as if to pay retribution but now there
was nothing he could do any more. Even his
students' agitation did not catch his attention
for some time. His stupor intensified, so did his
numbness.

On the island, madness was no laughing matter. It was
viewed as the gravest transgression, the worst illness.
They cast madmen into the sea from the top of the rocky
cliff on the other side of the island. In a land that knew almost no crime and only the lightest punishments, this

fierce attitude against madness was the one thing he could not agree with. The islanders, too, admitted the punishment was excessive, but refused to change it, arguing that upholding traditions was somehow indispensable to peace on the island.

He dismissed every single solution he could imagine: he simply had to get used to living with his heart-wrenching dilemma and he had to concede that icy indolence dictated the laws. Knowing all too well that this would be just escapism, and no solution, he decided to treat his money as the islanders treated madmen.

That evening, he climbed the hill and went to the rocky cliff. It felt as if the money, wrapped tightly in a handkerchief, were piercing his skin under his shirt. When he reached the top, he hesitated. Nobody would see him tossing money into the sea, true, but where would the waves carry the money? If someone found the money, others would certainly hear about it, and the prospect of being surrounded by gossip, of pretending innocent curiosity to avoid raising suspicion, terrified him. He decided to bury the money instead, amazed that he hadn't thought of it sooner. Taking out his pocketknife, he pried up a large stone, widened the hole underneath, and buried his money; he pushed the soil back into the hole and replaced the stone. Descending in the dark, he felt a great sense of satisfaction. After dinner, he sat in a café, worked a little, then went to bed. He slept deeply. In the morning, he opened the curtains closed against the mosquitoes and . . .

> At first, when he noticed the students' restlessness, he tried to tolerate their odd behavior and continue with the lesson, since he knew they worked hard and cared about learning. Soon, however, he wanted to know the reason for their

agitation, and trying not to appear too concerned, he asked them. All the children started
talking at once:

Early that morning, a student who lived in one of
the houses by the sea, the house right between
the bakery and the docks, had gone to fish for an
octopus—go get an octopus, his mother had told
him—the boy was very good at this, his mother
had already put the pot on the stove, the water
would boil by the time he returned, he went to
the bay, the same one he always went to between
Twin Rocks, though you wouldn't know it existed
because of the steep cliffs on both sides, but the
children—and we discovered it as children, too—
if you want, we can take you there, not that there
are a lot of fish but climbing the rocks is hard and
fun—and when the boy got there . . .

What he could gather was this:

When the boy got to the bay, he was startled: had he come
to the wrong place? The bay was full of dirt—the rocks that
rose above the water now rose above the soil. But the cliffs
on either side hadn't collapsed or anything; they remained
in place. The trees he knew, the brushwood he knew, they
were all in place. And the sea couldn't have simply receded:
the soil was dry and packed hard. When the boy returned
home, the water in the pot had been boiling a long time,
and his mother was angry at first and scolded him, but when
she heard what he had to say, she sent out the neighbor's
son who was three years older than him. When he returned, the neighbor's boy declared that the bay had vanished and then left in a hurry, rushing to tell his friends at
school. The woman was all the more perplexed because her
son told her he'd have to walk fifteen or twenty steps beyond the bay to reach the sea and catch an octopus.

He also drew the following conclusion:

The bay used to be narrow but deep. So it was unlikely that the sea could recede without anyone noticing and just as unlikely that strangers (or one stranger) could fill the bay. Since the trees and rocks were still in place, erosion was out of question.

"What do you think, Sir?" What could he think? Everything he'd been told had reached every other islander's ears within thirty minutes, or an hour at the most. Even as the students were entering his classroom, the island's leaders were sailing to inspect the bay from the sea. It would be best to reach a decision after the inspection.

That afternoon, nobody talked about anything else. Those who'd sailed out to inspect the bay had encountered the same situation in two other places. The sea was not receding at all. The new soil was hard, with almost no gravel or sand. It was also dry.

The needles on the earthquake station's most sensitive seismometers had not registered even the slightest tremor. In the face of this strange occurrence, those who'd grown accustomed to living with the fear of their island's destruction and had organized every aspect of their existence in case of such an eventuality stood speechless. Suddenly, a voice broke through the murmuring crowds in the harbor cafés. It was a sharp child's voice, although not loud. The child was standing beside the teacher. Everybody realized then that they'd been whispering because they were afraid. Perhaps what the child said was childish. "Our island is growing," he said. They hushed him. Later, when they went to bed, they felt more frightened than ever. Sleep did not come easily.

The teachers did not sleep that night; they searched their books and memories until daybreak. At dawn, they descended to the shore.

They had to believe their eyes. The sight surpassed

their worst fears: the docks still reached the sea but, on both sides, boats were set in the soil. The island seemed to be growing like a living creature, its body expanding in all directions.

In two days, the problem was identified: it was indeed a form of growth. It occurred at night and stopped during the day. The watchmen used high-powered flashlights and torches to investigate the phenomenon and witnessed the way a boat lingering in the water one moment was enveloped by a mass of dry soil the next. That was all they could see. The number of watchmen had to be increased, and they had to make sure they slept soundly during the day so they could remain alert on duty. But watches, diagnoses, the search for a solution, all this cost many precious days. On the morning of the third day, the islanders realized that they could not wait any longer. The sea in front of the docks began to disappear in places. They had to dig away the soil to salvage twelve fishing boats. Excavations took time; commerce was interrupted. On the fifth day, the cause of the growth was still unknown, and people began to throw malicious glances at anyone who'd thoughtlessly complained at one time or another about how small the island was. To be fair, more than a few people must have thought or said that their small island was indeed too small. And anyone bothered by these accusing glances countered with, "You, too, that day, don't you remember, during geography class . . . in the café . . . on the ship," trying to remind them of their own words—words that the accusers must have forgotten or perhaps never uttered.

The Councilmen issued a decree banning overconsumption of water and bread. They announced to the public that expert scientists had been summoned and would arrive in three days. The islanders became increasingly pessimistic about the possibility of finding a solution.

They had settled on this island before written history and, after centuries of fighting against the neighboring islands, had managed to create order. The memory of these events still survived in hazy fables and legends. Once a year, for seven consecutive evenings, they would gather on the largest sandbank and listen to the bards, who without forgetting a single word, revived the past through these fables and legends. The number of bards—seven—had not changed for centuries: each recited for one entire night. Since they were forbidden to repeat the same tale in successive years, each would complete the legend-cycle in seven years and begin again in the eighth year. In the middle of the second seven-year cycle, each bard would begin training a new pupil. The training would last about seventeen years. Any bard exhausted before daybreak had to relinquish his place to his pupil.

The island's growth sent the bards into turmoil as well. They had always ended their legends and fables at the point where the school history books began. But now, they wanted to seize the matter before the books did and avenge the mistreatment their words had received at the hands of history. History must end at this point. The words must belong to the bards and, when and if history resumed again, they would fill in the gap with their stories. In a mad effort, they began piecing together a new legend. The next festival would have to last eight days. An eighth bard would join them. They decided to train the lowest-ranking pupil, and not to worry about confusing his young mind. They would train him regardless.

Now the islanders decided to have a daytime meeting on the same sandbank. A meeting of students, teachers, fishermen, bakers, and water carriers who had left work for the occasion. The only people absent were the bards, or more precisely, the bards and their pupil . . . They could predict what would be discussed, or so they presumed. If a decision were reached, they would comply with it anyway. They needed to prepare the words that would recount the time after history came to an end.

Those who spoke at the gathering first summarized the bards' legends, then the accounts in history books; later, they expressed their feelings and thoughts concerning the island's expansion. Then the teachers reported on their research and observations to date and announced that they had started to search for preventive measures.

That's when fear stretched its red wings and began circling over the hills of the island.

There was no end to the speakers; the speeches became hurried and increasingly incomprehensible.

The expansion could incite greed among the neighbors; they could lose the new land; nothing good could come out of the growth: the islanders had lived for years planning against its dissolution; they could starve, die of thirst; they were not used to change; suddenly they were facing their limits; the dread of poverty seized them; if they failed to solve the problem, their forefathers would never forgive them; after all the disciplined work of so many years, would the ancestral land end up turning into a desert?

Everybody was speaking at once. The ancestors had established order. It could not be destroyed; it was being destroyed; it must not be destroyed.

It would be destroyed.

And when fear glided away like a red bird, disappearing beyond the hills, the chestnut horse of revolt stirred up a sandstorm and, reaching the shore, cast itself into the sea.

The shouts, "Order is being destroyed!" were swallowed by a vast silence that lasted a long time. Who had shouted this? The speakers had to come forth.

They were the sons of the oldest families on the hill: there were eight of them. They began speaking with one voice, each facing a different direction.

"Our esteemed bards toil to add a new legend to their

cycle. They struggle so that we won't forget our origins, but they don't join the meeting to save our island. We ask you, can people who behave in this way truly be concerned about the ancestral land?"

Silence followed. Over the years the bards had come to be seen as semi-sacred. The youngsters were charging them with a crime barely less than madness. This itself was madness.

"At best, they deserve our contempt," the young men jeered. And a wind of anger swept through the crowd. From all chests rose voices of derision that stirred the rocks and the soil.

"If the guards are sleeping, isn't the ancestral order bound for destruction?" asked the young men.

Another round of jeers followed, echoing through the land. The bards, sitting in their caves at the opposite end of the island, decided that the noise was too loud for them to keep on working; they took a ten-minute break from composing the fourth section of the fable they were preparing for the eighth evening.

"For three hours we have been talking here. Not a single boat has sailed, the dough has not been kneaded, and no one is attending to the ships approaching the harbor. How can the Council members who summoned us here claim to be concerned about the land?"

Ten Council members from the hill, another ten from the shore, and the three teachers' representatives to the Council, all looked at each other; drawing together, they began to say, "We . . . ," but, unprepared for jeers, they quickly collapsed, drowned out by the islanders.

"Enough!" shouted the youngsters. The crowd fell silent. "The bards and the Council have no power, as you've seen," they continued. "You were angry with us for shouting, 'It will be destroyed,' yet what hasn't been destroyed? Ask yourselves. Bakers, fishermen, water carriers, who among you had the good sense to say, 'Let's not all go to the gathering. Half us should stay behind and do our jobs'?"

Silence. Even the birds circling above them were frightened and flew away. Some of the workers lowered their heads and scurried back to the marketplace. The eight young men continued to accuse others, and as this went on, longer and longer, fewer and fewer people remained on the sandbank. The last few slowly grew confident that they would not be accused. The young men then began to soften their talk. They wanted to save the island from stagnation, from ancestral traditions that had proved vulnerable and no longer meaningful; they were determined to create a new understanding, a new way of thinking. To this end, they would seize control over everything, and cooperate with the only group that merited no accusations: the Research Team made up of eight teachers. Yet, the teachers should not overestimate this cooperation: they would merely provide guidance and conduct the necessary investigations.

That evening, the sixteen men put their heads together to discuss the state of the island and to debate solutions. First and foremost, they decided, the expansion had to be stopped. The eight teachers had no choice but to agree with the eight young men who made the decision. They were not about to disappoint their former students. Only this much was certain: none of their research and investigations had succeeded in illuminating the cause of the expansion. So what could be done? There were still fifty-seven hours before the experts were due to arrive. Not that it was certain that they would be able to do anything. When the young men increased the pressure on the teachers to come up with a solution, one of the teachers, perhaps feeling cornered, blurted out something to the effect that if they did not want the island to grow, it had to be halted, excavated. The young men responded with laughter. What was the teacher thinking?

But the teacher continued to speak—on what impulse even he didn't know—defending his proposal excitedly. From time to time, he would glance at his colleagues, his eyes asking for support. He was amazed at his own vigor. He described an elaborate excavation project, detail after fine detail, as if he had been thinking and planning for days. He did not worry whether his listeners found anything worthwhile in his words. Was his mind in charge, or was his tongue working on its own? He could not tell. Then, "That's it . . ." he said, and stopped, as if the spring of his mental clock had snapped unexpectedly.

He pulled himself together. Out of fear, he could not look at anybody and fixed his gaze on the floor. The silence that followed gave him courage. They were not laughing any longer. Clearly, they were considering his words. Raising his head, he came eye to eye with one of his colleagues. The vague smile breaking through the perplexed look made the familiar face somewhat alien to him.

How could he know that his friend was thinking of a broken glass, a buried pouch of money?

One of the youngsters broke the silence. "Let's adjourn, think carefully, and meet again in two hours to decide."

They adjourned.

> Money, glass, the island.
>
> But the island did not belong in the same string of words.
>
> His head was throbbing. He felt as though he were being forced to think in overused cliches, like "throbbing head." For the first time, he viewed madness, was able to view madness, in the rigid mold of the island's traditions. There was no point now in thinking like a teacher, in an educated, enlightened way. He had to be able to think like the rest of them, who knew noth-

ing, who *at this moment* knew nothing yet. But could he?

Even this was nonsense. Madness. Worse madness than the bards declaring that history had stopped. He had to start over.

The islanders had faced no difficulty until now. They had been able to live. Perhaps because of the feeling of transience they shared with their fear of earthquakes. And this expansion was the exact opposite of what they had feared and awaited. The exact opposite of perishing by crumbling: what they had hoped would not happen, and, as it had not happened for centuries, what they had slowly begun to believe (though they did not have the heart to tell anyone) would not happen. Just when they were becoming convinced that their worst quake fears would not be realized (though they acknowledged their conviction only now), they were facing something that had never even crossed their minds. A double disappointment of sorts. After spending centuries devising plans and measures against devastation, the best they could do now was to come up with one crazy idea. A solution that was even worse than the crazy, nonsensical one he had thought up a few days ago in order to get rid of his money—

He was sad that he could feel so detached, like a tourist who could leave the island whenever he wanted to. Not that he would. He had no place to return to. But that an unforeseen calamity could destroy the island—

But why destruction? Why didn't anyone seem to think of adjusting to the new condition? Perhaps this itself would be the cause of destruction. But to disclose his thoughts, to speak them out loud—

He could when the meeting resumed—

To perish in an unforeseen way like this would mean his own destruction as well. A dissolution. One that might even suit him.

When the group members reconvened, he asked to speak, and proposed his idea. They could wait to see whether the expansion would stop or not. Instead of using inadequate information to come up with a solution, when facing a natural phenomenon of unequaled character—

before his eyes paraded giant monstrous beasts, humans accustomed to hunger, or even worse, to a life that had lost its balance

to observe the occurrence closely and find a fitting solution—

The uproar overwhelmed his thoughts. When with great effort the young men calmed everyone down, he couldn't believe what he heard. It was obvious that he received little respect even as a teacher. His own students opposed him.

To begin with, everyone favored excavation, he had to accept this. Also, to be so indifferent to the fate of the island, as a stranger—

He did not want to hear the rest. If he could abandon everything and sail away with nothing but the shirt on his back—

Then again, the expanding land could be cultivated, the nature of our sea trade could change; besides in two days, the experts—

His desperate attempt was cut short by stern voices. "Either leave at once, or obey us and every one of our decisions."

He told them he would not leave.

His first job was to contact the experts. They were no longer needed. The islanders had already solved their problem themselves. Afterwards, the teacher was expected to join in the preparations for the excavation project.

He agreed. Why, he did not even want to know.

Before dusk, teams were assigned the task of excavating the island's docks, the three most important bays, and other areas where further land expansion would prove the most dangerous. The five-member teams would each work for three hours, and the shifts would last through the night.

The next morning, when the workers rested, the fishermen sailed off easily, and the ships carrying flour docked and unloaded easily. The water carriers were able to transport water up the hill. The island returned to life.

In the Council room, the young men and the teachers had pushed the extra chairs to a corner and were sitting more comfortably than the old Council had. There was no avoiding the vainglory of the teacher who had first proposed the idea of excavation. Since the solution seemed successful, the group wanted to attend to other matters. In two hours, all matters were settled.

The group met again in the afternoon and received neighborhood delegates who wanted to express their joy. Later, the group decided to increase the number of excavation teams and dig out other expanded areas.

On the morning of the third day, the Executive Committee, for so they called themselves, sat in the meeting room and waited to receive news of final victory. No one showed up. Toward noon, after finishing work, the members adjourned somewhat disappointedly. Yet, what they heard brought them back together within less than an hour. On account of the additional excavation teams, daily work on the island had been interrupted. The sandbank where all the residents had gathered was transformed into a vast plateau because no excavation work had been done there. After weighing options, some islanders ventured: "Let's farm the land. It could be profitable." Who gave them that idea, others asked. The teacher was accused, threatened, told that his punishment would be severe if he encouraged such thinking. At the same time, no one wanted to be too harsh with him since, after much debate, all admitted that the idea of cultivating the land was not so outlandish as to require outside provocation. Nevertheless, it was officially declared on behalf of the Committee that participating in the excavation effort was, for the time being, a more pressing duty than farming. And thus the initiative was suppressed. In the evening, fishermen returning from the sea reported that boats from surrounding islands were sailing disturbingly close to the island. There was nothing startling about this, they were told. As the island widened, it was growing nearer the other islands.

It was decided that work would continue around the clock and the teams would be organized to remain on duty day and night; fewer workers would be responsible for the daily business of the island; shifts would be increased from three to six hours; and, given the general fatigue induced by such intense labor, minor interruptions in daily routines would have to be tolerated.

The Executive Committee had no time to assess whether its thinking was sound.

The island was now growing during the day as well.

The teachers on the Committee proposed that the schools be closed. In turn, the eight young men asked the hill residents to move into tents that would be set up on the shore. This way, services would be provided more easily.

In four days, the pickaxes no longer proved adequate for the task. One of the teachers designed a machine that would excavate in one hour what it took ten people three hours to dig. With the limited resources available, however, only three machines could be constructed, provided that twenty-nine people worked twelve-hour shifts for three days. The work started immediately.

Disposing the excavated soil and rocks in the sea was, of course, out of the question. That much was clear. Initially, the workers had tried to load the excess soil in boats and ferry it to the open sea, but as that soon proved unmanageable, they began to transport it to the uninhabited rocky area behind the town. Now, when they looked up from their work, they saw all around them strange new formations: tall mounds of soil overtaking the terrain.

The Executive Committee saw no reason to impose rigid rules on top of those governing steady labor. But the edict issued on the morning of the twelfth day was quite shocking. It prohibited all forms of sexual activity: for obvious reasons, it stated, the island's population must remain unchanged until the situation is brought under control. More importantly, at a time when the residents must work two six-hour shifts daily, they have to resist the demeaning frailty of sexual desire and preserve their energy for the solemn and pressing task of digging.

The people were perplexed by this edict. The meeting of two people at home, in the same room, had already become nearly impossible. The very young children had been put on alarm-clock duty and were required to wake up the adults for their shifts. Day after laborious day divided between digging and six hours of sleep had brought the islanders near to complete exhaustion.

By the time the machines were ready, they had to be used not to excavate but to push the spreading mounds of excess soil farther away from the shore.

People dug and dug, finding no time to notice their surroundings. Because of the mounds piling up around them, they did not leave the work site at breaks but curled up asleep wherever possible. Nothing was in sight but the ever-rising mounds.

On the morning of the fourteenth day, one of the machines was taken to the shore to demolish the first row of houses that used to overlook the sea.

The ongoing investigations—who was conducting them, no one knew, except perhaps the Executive Committee members since the diggers saw no one but the other diggers—the ongoing investigations confirmed that the expansion was worst by the mansions along the shore (that is, what used to be the shore). Therefore, the work would have to concentrate on that area.

While the demolition of houses continued, the hill (its outline gradually disappearing among the rising mounds) was washed by the terrific roar of the other two machines.

That evening, the workers noticed the sound slowly dimming, as if traveling into heavy fog; they stopped digging and clawed their way up over the mounds. They were surprised to see the machines still working away at full speed. As night descended, they realized that they had lost much of their hearing and were almost deaf. "Because of the noise of the machines," they told themselves and continued digging.

The next morning, they worked in perfect silence. Each was now as deaf as a post. To their right, to their left, the mounds continued to pile up: the sole evidence that others were still working. Food tents were set up close to the work sites. When the shifts ended, the workers would go to eat before sleeping or trying to look after their own business, that is, if they were near enough. For those stationed far away, there was nothing to do but dig. They still changed shifts, but among the mounds, finding their way around or locating the food tents became increasingly difficult. Each passing day, there was less and less to eat with less and less taste to it.

Shifts were stepped up again; rest became little more than a promise on paper. Aside from the written directives that somehow always reached the work sites, communication ceased. People had neither the time nor the energy to try to understand one another.

They were asked to work harder and harder, to sleep and rest on the site and then plunge themselves back into work. No time could be wasted on the road; children would deliver food. This was the last written directive also broadcast on the radio: the radio employees were probably the only ones on the island who still had their hearing. Yet, because exactly who could still hear was never determined, the radio announcement was repeated a few times daily.

On the third day of deafness, one of the workers died while operating the excavation machine on a steep incline. He fell to the ground, as though struck by lightning. It was a heart attack. The workers had moved the machine to this site, after demolishing the shoreline houses. The death did not cause confusion at the worksite because an official directive had already spelled out the correct procedure. His friends buried him reasonably well under a nearby mound, assigned another worker to operate the machine, and promptly returned to their tasks. They worked until a little girl arrived with their meal. They sent her back with the news that they were one fewer. Toward evening, as the team began its second shift, the teacher arrived as the replacement. The workers were very intrigued: had it been decided that the Executive Committee members, too, had to work, or had the teacher been sent for another reason? But they didn't ask; they had no time to ask.

The teacher didn't tell his teammates that, three days ago, the rocky cliff behind the island had collapsed under the mass of excavated soil heaped on it; that part of the hill

below the cliff had caved in, destroying an entire neighborhood along with the schools; and that many had died,
trapped under the avalanche. There was no way of knowing the extent of the devastation—the only place from
which the entire island could be seen had become un-
reachable since the landslide. Having run out of measures
to enact, the Executive Committee decided to assign its
members to the teams so they could both work and assess
firsthand the state of the shoreline. It wasn't even clear
whether the Committee would reconvene after the assess-
ment was complete. But the teacher did not mention any
of this. Besides, no one could hear well enough to understand. The Executive Committee was deaf now, like everybody else.

When the little girl who brought their meal did not
show up in the evening, they weren't worried. Perhaps she
would be a little late, or perhaps they were feeling hungry
sooner than usual. Having nothing else to do, they worked
until it started to get dark. When the girl didn't come,
they opened their reserve supply and ate one ration. They
decided when it was pitch dark that sleeping would be the
sensible thing to do and lay on the ground.

At daybreak, the teacher woke up, his body aching all
over, as if people had been beating him up all night. He noticed the sharp smell of wet soil and picked up his pickax.
No one was in sight, no one was bringing food. Should he
try to find the food tent? He was reluctant and took out his
second ration and ate it. The mounds of freshly dug soil appeared to have found new shapes overnight. As he ate, staring around drowsily, he could see that they'd changed but
couldn't pinpoint exactly how. And he was so exhausted!
His feet were wet; he didn't even wonder why the others
hadn't woken him up . . . And after beginning to dig, he
noticed that none of his team members was around. The
mounds had changed shape but not by expanding, he was

sure of that. Circling a couple of them, he saw the tips of a few pickaxes and two or three pairs of feet. His friends were trapped underneath.

He remembered the silent movies. Again. The silent movie shows in his youth, faint music serving to remind those watching that they weren't deaf. When the rocky cliff collapsed, nobody had heard the roaring fall or felt any tremor. They had discovered the devastation afterwards. This particular landslide, too, must have come silently—of course—without tremors . . . Anyway, it wasn't unusual not to feel tremors; the soil was loose. Why had he escaped death? He wanted to understand, but he hesitated. He would continue digging instead.

Then the sun was high, his arms were spent.

For days (or was it hours, he couldn't tell) he'd had no time to think. Now he could rest and think.

The landslide had missed him; obviously, the soil had slid toward the sea. The other workers must have fallen asleep closer to the water. Quite possible, it seemed. He tried to envision how they looked the last time he saw them. He'd fallen asleep farther back, on top of a mound, and slept through the first rays of sunshine; he woke up only when his feet got wet. Now the water was up to his ankles. The mounds seemed to be dissolving; staring blankly, he noticed that the water was rising.

He was exhausted to the point of not wondering whether or not he should be afraid. He tried clambering over the heaps of loose soil, away from the sea, away from the approaching water, and was surprised to find that he could move without too much effort. He was walking, but the sea was following him.

Apparently, the expansion had stopped. The excavation project had reached its goal, and perhaps exceeded it. He managed a vague smile.

From where he stood, he could see the entire coastline. All of it. He must have reached the top of the hill.

The hill that had disappeared among the rising mounds of soil. All around, he could see mounds collapsing, toppling, dissolving. The water was fast approaching. A flat stone emerging from the soil caught his eye. He went and sat on the stone. He felt dizzy. The water ebbed and flowed, loosening more of the soil around the stone. Suddenly among the wavelets he noticed paper bills floating. In the corner of his mouth, he felt a sharp twinge. Perhaps these were his bills. The money he had buried a few weeks ago. Or perhaps they belonged to someone else. . . .

The twinge came again.

Now his knees were in the water. Around him, the sea spread endlessly, almost calm. The water rose to his waist. He didn't move.

A torso, and then, just a head. The only thing left behind, but not for much longer . . .

1971–1975

10.

I think the mayor favored me. He was protecting me from the most dangerous offensives, sparing me while sacrificing others, and steadily moving me toward the Vizier.

Fewer players remained. Perhaps half of us were still in the game.

The Greens defended themselves brilliantly. They were skillful players. He and I continued staring at each other. As if extending them toward me, he moved his arms, and then he smiled, swinging his arms down and hitting his fists against his thighs.

I was thirsty. We all must have been, and we couldn't forget that we were fighting for water. There would be no water until the end.

All I knew about the game I had learned from him, my master standing before me. But he hadn't explained how the game was played. It resembled chess, the pieces had the same names, and the rules were almost identical, though with a couple of exceptions that the mayor had told me about this morning. Yet, no one had asked me if I knew how to play chess. (The Purples didn't have to know anyway.) Neither did I try to excuse myself by saying I didn't know since I had played some chess in the past. I had been intent on playing from the start, ever since I met him and he asked me if I would play.

Neither did he explain the name, "The Game of Departures." I could now call this place The Garden of the Departed, but I had come up with the name long before I knew anything about the game. Something else occurred to me: This was not the garden of the departed; rather, it was a garden where old cats came to die in peace, away from the eyes of the living. This was the Garden of the Departed Cats.

Our eyes met again. As if privy to my thoughts, he nodded, "Yes," with a slightly mocking smile. The mayor was still contemplating his next move. I began to play my own game.

You can let me live, I thought to myself.

Again, he nodded "Yes."

But you don't want to because you

His face asked, "Yes?"

Want to know that you are loved.

Yes.

But you want it to remain unspoken. You can drown me in unspoken love.

Yes.

Because . . .

Because?

I don't know. Perhaps. . . . You're afraid.

Yes.

I stopped playing. He was getting annoying.

He didn't stop.

I am still waiting, he said. . . .

Give it up, I said, gesturing with my head. The mayor coughed. I must have moved. I froze.

I hadn't even looked at the cat that rubbed itself against my legs before walking back to the trees, where it disappeared, hungry, or perhaps tired. It must have died. Departed from this garden.

The mayor forgot me, and I, a lowly pawn . . .

(he was now defending other pieces)

. . . and I, a meager pawn, was thinking of no one else but the Vizier. What should I do. . . .

But as far as I was concerned the game was over. One move on my part would bring everything to an end. No need for "what should I do" any more. I wasn't a skilled player, but the move was perfectly obvious, and my satisfaction almost certain.

There was another stirring in the field. Where, why, I didn't know. But I knew it was my turn.

Everything stood still, waiting for me, and I was waiting to hear the word from the mayor who remained silent, thinking. He couldn't give any other order, it was clear. My entire body tensed up, ready to attack. In one move, I'd be challenging the Green's Vizier. He'd have no choice, he'd be mine. . . .

With his green eyes, he spoke to me, as if saying "No." As if pleading.

No to what?

To what you're thinking.

Don't be absurd—we're at the point of no return. Of course you wouldn't want me to take you.

No, that's not it . . .

He wanted to talk without derision, without assuming superiority, without belittling me. I had to read his mind just as he read mine. The Green wanted peace but not the Purple. I was using all my strength to decipher him.

No, he said. What you're thinking is wrong.

I was surprised. He was distracting me. He had figured out my intentions and was trying to stop me. We were enemies.

Hadn't we been friends until today? Hadn't we sat face to face?

From the first time we met, he had enchanted me. Was it all an illusion?

I didn't want to give up my resolve. I stopped looking at him and watched the mayor for his command. He made his decision and opened his mouth.

I didn't wait for the words and took a single big step—the spectators gasped.

When they calmed down, I heard his voice. "Checkmate." I collapsed. With my shield and my tools, I collapsed amid the thundering sound of iron.

Since every hunchback's family is a tad poetic
Brace him up and he can be his own apprentice
To revive dead words and children
Each time a march is replayed on this earth
Do not forget the hunchback
Who is his own master, his own apprentice
—E. Ayhan "The State and Nature"

RED-SALAMANDER *

To Haluk Aker

1.

His back to the window, he stood in front of them. The curtains saturated the room with a crimson-tinged darkness, but he was still able to see distinctly the faces of both his mother and his mother's friend. His mother's face showed both anger and surprise, an expression he had never seen before. Her friend's face showed a smile and surprise. Both were staring at him.

When he raised his head—when he had to, that is—and looked, he always noticed something strange in people's faces. And he found the faces of the passersby on the street—when he caught a glimpse of them—dull and ordinary, like the faces of sleepers, betraying none of their worries, except that the ones on the street had their eyes open and their mouths—more often than not—closed.

---

*Don't try to search the dictionary. Even if you find it, this flower is a fabrication.

Each time this contrast occurred to him, he quickly shrugged it off.

"Now I have to bring them out and show your Aunt Refika," his mother said. "Otherwise, she'll think I am lying." He couldn't understand anything. His mother left, then returned: in her hand were his dark-blue shoes—which he knew well and liked. "So there," he said, looking at his mother, "these aren't boots, I'm right, aren't I? Aren't I right?" Aunt Refika said, "They call this style half-boots, my dear child." "See?" his mother said, "you should never meddle in things you don't understand and talk as if you do; don't call truth a lie or a lie truth. Don't ever lie."

Lies were bad. Lies were forbidden. His parents had patiently instilled in him the habit of hiding nothing, of telling them what he broke or ripped, yet at the same time they'd tried to teach him that it was impolite to voice, to reveal, his every thought. One could say that he had started sensing at an early age the boundary between truths that could be voiced and truths that couldn't; however, as he grew older and learned that it wasn't enough to sense this boundary, he also lost hope in ever being able to draw a sharp line between them.

He was around sixteen when one day, he shaved his head, saying, "I should look the way I am." He later realized that, with or without hair, the face he saw in the mirror was his; he was always himself. But in the eyes of others, his two modes were much too different, and his true self all the harder to determine. He gave up and started visiting the barbershop every other week just so his shaven and unshaven looks were at least similar.

What is truth? What is a lie? Seeking answers to these questions, he first studied philosophy then psychology, and later gained expertise in the science of the human brain, investigating its minutest functions; all along, he continued to explore any field of knowledge closely—or remotely—concerned with the problem of truth versus falsehoods. His studies yielded many worthwhile findings. Still, he felt caught in an endless chase. One concept sent him to another, one field to the next, but he remained undeterred. And beyond—or beside—all his research, he still knew that he had to continue living his everyday life, which meant constantly living truthfully.

But he was the first to recognize that it's very easy to deceive one's self: He always weighed his words and deeds, thinking that even while attempting to speak the truth, he could deceive himself and consequently others. He always checked himself. He tried to describe exactly what he saw, resisting as much as he could elegant interpretations that could be false, exaggerated or misleading; he owned up to what he did and what he didn't do.

He immersed himself in the study of old books and manuscripts, and grew accustomed to ingesting library dust while searching for the wisdom of the ancients; he had stepped into a different world that existed beyond— and before—all the experiments conducted on live animal brains, beyond all logic, linguistics, mathematics, and all the sciences. Some of the claims deserved scrutiny, and others merely ridicule. However, all those ancient writers who bequeathed their wisdom to future generations seemed surprisingly confident; it was a straightforward, naïve, unadulterated confidence. Frankly, he could understand why scientists less charitable than himself ridiculed these claims. Perhaps everyone liked inventing stories, in the past and today. People readily believed these stories even though they doubted the events unfolding right in front of them or words spoken to their faces— truth was different, they insisted, very different from what it seemed; and if reality didn't match the stories they'd invented, then, in their eyes, it was not the stories but reality that was lying. Perhaps all people were the same. Or people "in general." After all, you could always depend on the enigmatic power of "in general." Had he not been taught that very few people considered plainly spoken truths "elegant"?

If asked, he would have probably said that the sea was truthful: this was his poetic side. If asked why the sea was truthful, he would have probably found it difficult to explain. And was he drawing a connection between the sea and his mother who had instilled truthfulness in him—even though she had also taught him facts that were, if not false, at least inaccurate or incomplete? He'd never ventured to answer this question.

In one of the old books—a thirteenth-century study on medicinal plants—he came upon a plant he had previously heard of but never read about. He was quite astonished by the finely detailed description of the plant's characteristics and its uses.

Nearly everyone in his country loved flowers and growing plants. You could count on your fingers the few who didn't grow a plant—flowering or not—in a container, whether an oil can or an earthen pot. Every flower and plant was considered beautiful, but the rose was loved the most.

It was common knowledge: for centuries, and even today, old wives' cures were made mostly from plant extracts, and—once found beneficial—never forgotten throughout the villages and the cities. Yet the plants grown for pleasure and those with medicinal properties—even when identical—held a different place in people's hearts.

Wasn't the most poignant example of this the distinction made between a tulip's flower and its bulb? The bulb you could find everywhere: there was a particular way to cultivate it, a particular way to dry and crush it; and it was mixed with powders of different leaves as a balm for various kinds of itches. Yet the flower, burdened with a history of animosity, had become something almost—almost—forgotten, unknown, unseen.

Strangely enough, the plant described in the thirteenth-century book on medicinal plants was also of a bulbous variety.

Its white—or yellowish white—shiny, large, bellshaped flowers bloomed along sandbanks, deserted seashores, in sands undisturbed by animals or humans; for some reason, the plant was called red-salamander. The book pointed out that the flower was very fragrant, but that, once plucked, it shriveled and disintegrated. The bulb was very effective against itching when dried and pounded together with certain dried leaves. The book also added that, probably due to the sea salt or the undisturbed soil in its natural habitat, the plant's leaves had significant powers. People were known to have gone insane after chewing the two blade-like leaves rising from the base of the long stem that carried the flower. Since the writer added that those who chewed on a third leaf turned stonecold and died, two reasons could explain why some of the insane ate the lethal third leaf. Either they acted on instinct, and managed, in a way, to escape insanity, or they found this state of insanity so sweet that they wished to intensify it. Clearly, there was no time left for a fourth leaf. Yet, why even chew a second leaf? The book somehow hinted at an explanation—of sorts—in the last line of the section dedicated to the plant: Ingesting only one leaf made people incapable of telling a lie.

Once he read this, he enjoyed no more sleep or rest; like a madman, he rummaged through countless old libraries and corresponded with librarians outside the city. Besides what he already knew, he learned nothing else that was useful. Only one book mentioned the name, redsalamander, noting: "In ancient times, there were red salamanders, born of fire, living in fire. They were so rare that no one believed in their existence. The few who did see them preferred to remain silent, either because no one believed them or because they didn't believe their own eyes. Since no one believed in their existence and they were al-

lowed only to live in fairy tales, in time these salamanders
were beset by unimaginable sorrow. Consequently, obey-
ing the oldest among them, the salamanders each ate a leaf
of a certain flower; their color changed, and they turned
into ordinary salamanders. And the old sages who had witnessed this agreed on the fairest name for the fair flower,
calling it the red-salamander. Since that time, the flower
has been known by that name . . ." (This information
was from an eleventh-century book that contained nothing but brief descriptions of rare flowers. The director of
the library that carried the book had transcribed all of the
above, then politely asked in his letter: "May I please inquire about the reason of your interest in this subject?"
And how fiercely the scientist had struggled, while writing
to thank the director, to offer nothing more than a trivial
explanation for his keen interest . . .)

It would have been easy enough to dismiss all this as a
fairy tale, but the scientist found one thing thoroughly
confounding: in consuming a single leaf of the plant, the
red salamanders (that is, the animals) had forfeited their
nature—in one sense, their truth—and conformed to what
humans deemed to be truth. The origin of truth, according to this fairy tale, was the human eye. And what about
the helpless honesty of those who ingested a single leaf?
Was their truth the selfsame truth of all stories invented
by humans?

He prepared for his expedition and set out to find pristine sandbanks. Abandoning all the wires thrust into the
live animal brains, all the debates and the scientific confer-
ences, leaving everything to the care of his assistants and
students . . .

He was going to start with the southern shores. Since
these desolate sandbanks could only be accessed from the
sea, he hired two men and a boat. Both of the men were
praised for their seamanship; he was told that they knew
the coast like the back of their hands. He explained exactly

what he was looking for and where he hoped to find it; they must have understood him—before the end of the second day, they'd found him three different sandbanks.

But they bore no trace of the red-salamander.

On the fourth day and the eighth sandbank, he found what he was looking for, and quite frankly, he was a little surprised that he wasn't surprised at all. He wanted to believe his eyes. "You see what I see, don't you?" he asked the boatmen who were a little perplexed. When someone finds what he's looking for, why wouldn't he believe his eyes? They chuckled at his question, thinking that he was perhaps overexcited. If these were indeed red-salamanders, there were five plants. Ten leaves. Enough to kill all three of us, he thought—and the one remaining leaf could just take its time to wither and crumble beside their corpses. But even thinking of this joke was uncalled for.

First and foremost, to avoid disturbing the plant, he had to examine it without getting too close. Through his binoculars, he saw that the plant was indeed the one described and identified in that old book. He knew the text by heart. He put on the protective suit and mask he'd ordered specially for the occasion, waded ashore and approached one of the plants. Straining to take quiet and light steps, he hoped to avoid—if not entirely, then as much as possible—damaging the plant. He plucked the flower and, turning his back to the other flowers, he pulled off his mask to smell it. What the book described as very beautiful smelled to him, at the most, like a very beautiful sea, and in a matter of seconds, the flower shriveled and disintegrated, blowing away like dust. He turned again to the plant he'd plucked the flower from; very carefully, he first removed its leaves, and then he dug up its bulb caked with sand, placing it inside the special container he'd ordered and brought along with him, and then he carried them to the boat. He removed his mask and protective suit, and offering each boatman a leaf, he asked whether they would like to eat it. (The first day, when he had enumerated all the properties of the plant he was looking for, they'd laughed and said: "There is no such thing! How could we never have heard of it?" But then they had added, "You find it and we'll be happy to eat it, we promise!") The two hesitated at first, but then ate the leaves. They even went so far as to declare that they tasted very sweet. Before too long, they said they were feeling drowsy, and had to lie down.

The scientist reproached himself for trusting information found in an ancient book—how could he have been so stupid as to believe that just one single leaf would not harm these men? How, yes he was caught in the excitement of a new discovery, but how could he have behaved so thoughtlessly and—why not say it—so immorally? Was it enough to have told the men the truth from the beginning, especially when they clearly hadn't believed him?

Nothing could be done. Let them sleep for now.

It was getting dark. Putting on his mask and protective suit again, he went to collect the rest of the plants and their bulbs. He placed them in their containers and carried them back to the boat. Then he sat beside the sleepers and decided to wait until morning. If something happened to them, what would he do, what could he do? He didn't know. But nothing happened. With the arrival of dawn, they cheerfully woke up and stretched. "We're going back," he told them; he wanted to return to his laboratory at once and begin examining the plants. He lay down and fell asleep.

In his dream, he saw himself cultivating red-salamanders. He was distributing the leaves—one leaf, always one leaf at a time—among his friends and the passersby on the streets, feeding them and then returning to his laboratory. The laboratory environment re-created the small, deserted, breezy sandbanks outlined by sea water and rocks, and provided everything, everything, including the perfectly quiet and pristine conditions free of the trace of any living beings. Harvesting red-salamanders, he was feeding the leaves—one leaf, always one leaf at a time—to everyone, to every adult, child and infant, who lived in the land. But then, quite by mistake, he began to distribute the leaves in twos and threes, and was watching people eat the leaves. He woke up in a panic, drenched in sweat and gasping. The boatmen had opened all the special containers and eaten all the leaves: he wanted to scream but his voice failed him. He leapt at them, but with a flick—a single flick—of the finger, the men tossed him into the sea. The boat was moving away: he tried swimming; the water was icy. Exhausted, he kept being drawn under the waves. He swallowed water, sank, struggled to the surface, and then he experienced the euphoria of drowning in every fiber of his body; his torment was already over. How quickly! The last thing he saw was a tulip field. He was struggling among tulips engulfing his entire body. With the last of his strength, he tried to rip apart the tulip stems strangling him. His hands hit against the hard wood. Light pierced his eyes. He closed them, but little by little he opened them again. The boatmen were standing over him.

"You were having a bad dream," one of them said. "We're approaching the harbor," the other said. The scientist tried to sit up. Collecting himself took a lot of effort, and it wasn't until they entered the harbor that he found the strength to check the red-salamanders in their special containers. He wanted to pay the boatmen. One of them smiled, "I am no boatman," he said, "I wasn't supposed to tell you, but I was assigned to protect you, that's why I was sent to come along." The other smiled also. "I wasn't supposed to tell you either, but my charge was to moni-tor your activities," he said, "I imagine you'll agree that a scientist like yourself needs to be both protected and monitored . . ."

He was quite perplexed, but after a while he thought that, perhaps, the old book's description of the leaves' effects was being confirmed before his eyes. He merely smiled. "In that case," he said, "you should accompany me and my flowers to my laboratory. I couldn't find better assistants than you." He had known that people were watching him from afar, but he had never seen them closely until today.

First they took a train, then a plane. In the evening, he began examining the red-salamanders.

• • •

Telling no lies, telling the truth. From the beginning, these were separate matters, even though they were presented as equivalent injunctions. In education as well as in every stage of life, the two together were viewed as cardinal virtues. Yet nowadays, to truly not lie—and more so, to really tell the truth—was perceived almost as a shortcoming in the everyday life of trivial affairs. Did he not know this from the beginning? Hadn't he been criticized enough on this account?

At one point, he had thought, "Since everyone has a shortcoming, let this one be mine," and tried to dodge the whole issue. But it wasn't possible. What really mattered wasn't whether you didn't lie or you only told the truth, but convincing everyone else that you possessed the virtue of truthfulness. Those who criticized his truthfulness accused him of being, in reality, a liar. They told him outright: "In reality, you are a liar." Of course, always in everyday life. Outside everyday life, the truth-untruth duality assumed the guises of misjudgment, criticism, objective fact, stirring endless disputes. True, among those who called him a liar, or implied as much, were some who—to their credit—tactfully explained that "the most masterful lies are those told in the guise of truths," and that he had become "one of the greatest masters of this art."

If he were asked, he would say his real shortcoming was this:

Seldom, if ever, did it occur to him that someone could be lying to him. Yes, certain circumstances forced one to lie. For instance, there was no sense in telling a dying man, "You're dying, you only have a few hours left." Just because that was the truth did not require one to display such poor taste—as in volunteering an answer to an unasked question. Yet, being asked a question should not in itself require one to concoct lies and pretend to know what one does not. Why lie? He was therefore ready to believe everything he was told. His principal shortcoming was his tendency to compartmentalize the needs of everyday life, on the one side, and his scientific skepticism and everything he'd learned through psychology, on the other. Wasn't "credulity" one of the bricks with which his friends—those who called him a liar or implied as much—beat him on the head, again ever so tactfully? He had therefore decided some time back that the best course of action was to trust science with its most objective method. The day would surely arrive when objective science would overlap with everyday life . . . Perhaps this, too, was optimism, and a naïve, credulous form of optimism at that. But who had been able to purge himself of all shortcomings? True, preeminently superior individuals did exist. He just wasn't one of them.

Yet, he wasn't mistaken when he chose to believe—rather than disbelieve—in a thirteenth-century book. He found the plant. Later, he didn't hesitate feeding the leaves to the boatmen—even though the warning in the book warranted hesitation at least. (And the men, did they cheerfully eat the leaves because they were duty-bound and, risking their lives, wanted to test whether the plant possessed all the properties described in the book? Or was it because they didn't believe him at all?) If the men were visibly harmed, wouldn't he appear to have acted like a fool? With this line of reasoning, science and everyday life would never, could never, unite . . . How much further would science have to crawl before deciding whether to speak the truth or to remain silent?

• • •

While trying to cultivate red-salamander plants in a laboratory environment, he also worked at deciphering the chemical compound of the leaf of this plant entirely unknown to contemporary botany. Venturing to take into account not only the compounds in the leaf, but also the new ones that form during the process of chewing or digestion . . . After a point, the study would also have to involve experiments. For two months, the laboratory work proceeded with the utmost secrecy: the six-member research team—including the two boatmen—explored alternative methods of investigation, pursuing various clues at once. And in utmost secrecy the members prepared themselves for the day when they would have enough evidence to attempt limited experiments with very small dosages.

• • •

One morning, he found a letter on his table; it came from the library director who had sent him the information on the red-salamander found in the eleventh-century book.

Leafing through this very interesting book now and again, the director had ended up reading all of it, even though the prose was difficult to follow. Whether the esteemed scientist would be interested in the book's various legends and fables about plants, the director didn't know, but it would probably behoove him to seize the first opportunity and visit the city and its old library.

Here, he raised his head from the letter. The small city he had never seen slowly began taking shape before his eyes: the dusty streets, the residents, indifferent, watching the reckless demolition of some old buildings while restoration work slowly continued on a few others, the library safeguarded by an old wall and a new iron fence . . . The library director—could be young or old—had to be someone who loved the books stacked along the shelves, lamenting that they were seldom read, and scolding the schoolchildren sent to the library to study but who did little beside whispering and giggling—although he must issue only mild, teacherly reproaches, lest the children, too, stop coming, altogether condemning the library to desolation. He was probably hoping to use the occasion of a scientist's query from the capital as an opportunity to promote first the library, then himself, and in the end, to obtain some benefit for the library, and who knows, perhaps also for himself . . . The scientist smiled. He placed a paperweight on the letter, locked his office door, and following his assistant who had come to call him, he went to review the first set of data that the computer had just produced.

• • •

The findings were noteworthy, suggesting progress toward the discovery of two hitherto unknown compounds. Having had to weigh various probabilities, the analyses entailed the most precise methods of investigation. Concurrently, the team had to begin experimental research on animals, though anticipating very rudimentary results, at best . . . Perhaps much later (or perhaps soon), it would be possible to conduct experiments on human subjects . . .

When he returned to his desk and noticed the letter he had left under the paperweight, he felt tired and hungry. On his way to lunch, he tried imagining the rest of the letter that he planned to read while drinking his coffee. He offered absentminded smiles to his friends and acquaintances returning from the cafeteria. His mental picture of the library director gradually assumed a gray countenance complete with a long beard matched by a body warped with age. Incapable of shaking the book dust off his clothes, the old man . . . But no, he couldn't be old—both his language and his handwriting were young; this man who could readily admit to the difficulties of reading old manuscripts had to be young. Or maybe not— the scientist put his hand in his pocket, then changed his mind again about the director's age. The guessing-game would last until his coffee arrived. The young director was probably dying to impress the scientist, perhaps to achieve fame and professional advancement by providing an invaluable service. Nothing strange about that. Yet—

The meal arrived. Then, a garrulous colleague disturbed his solitude, and he worried that he wouldn't be able to read the letter when his coffee was served. After considerable effort, he managed to shoo the man away.

He had guessed right. The director had noted that he was thirty years old. He had distinguished himself early in life; was the mention of his age intended to suggest that he was not an ordinary person? Yet he sounded almost apologetic: "Because, at thirty, as I read this old manuscript to the extent my training allows . . ." Immediately following was the letter's most interesting detail: "Would you believe it? Even the legend of the tulip field is described as *a fairy tale* . . ."

The words "tulip field" suddenly threw him back to the eerily lifelike dream he had had while on the boat.

This young director he had never seen and perhaps would never see was suddenly sending his mind, his entire being, into turmoil.

He decided not to finish the letter and put it in his pocket. He wasn't going to read the last two pages. No matter what they contained . . . But he would write a response. Short and unequivocal.

That evening, sitting in his comfortable armchair, in the solitude of home, his thoughts took a sudden turn.

The legend of the tulip field seized hold of him and carried him away. But along with the legend, something else,
something else . . . Something that eluded him but was
making him anxious nonetheless . . . The legend, as far
as he knew and could remember, went something like this:

Once there was a warlord. Victorious in battle after
battle, his fame had begun to alarm even the emperor
himself. The warlord had imposed tariffs on all neighboring states. One day, the news reached his capital that one
of the states—and the smallest one at that—was repeatedly attacking one of the rich border villages of his do-
main, looting its oil, wheat and wealth. The warlord summoned his army and charged toward the enemy state.
At the border, he came upon a huge tulip field and he
wouldn't allow his horses to trample the flowers (at the
time, the tulip was much loved, considered almost sacred
throughout the land); and while his men rode around
the field, the enemy cavalry noticed the detour, and in-
vaded the defenseless village, burning and razing it to the
ground. Consequently, the warlord was beheaded, but it
took two hundred years before life in the village returned
to normal and borders became secure and stable again in
that region.

In time the warlord was forgotten but the anger he'd
aroused must have been then directed toward the tulip: for
centuries after this event (as both history books and fairy
tales attest), it was absolutely forbidden to grow tulips.
Those permitted to cultivate tulip bulbs for medicinal
purposes were licensed, while those fond of growing flowers were told to grow roses instead. Although no one was
growing tulips anymore, the antagonism intensified rather
than abated with time, spreading from the plant to its
figurative representations. Wherever a tulip figure was
found, it was quickly effaced or removed, and replaced
with a rose. For a long time, many families of artisans
earned their living by practicing the craft of tulip-effacing

and rose-engraving. (Still—as with all types of prohibition—there was a widespread rumor that, over the centuries, some people had disregarded the prohibition and secretly cultivated tulips . . . Did these people merely dislike prohibitions, or were they born with a love of tulips or with a sense of helpless inseparability from the flower? This was a topic of everlasting debate.)

Centuries had passed since, but the tulip had remained unforgiven. From time to time, tulip lovers had wished to declare their love and not to feel ashamed for loving the flower, but some were persecuted while others were appointed as directors at rose gardens and nurseries, where they spent the rest of their lives—that is, when they weren't fired, framed or banished to remote places . . .

The legend behind the legend . . . All this was fine, interesting enough, but something else seemed to flow alongside these thoughts; something else that made him anxious . . .

• • •

The letter was supposed to be short and unequivocal, but for a long time the scientist could not write it. One morning he found on his desk another letter from the young library director.

The work at the laboratory had slowed down recently. They were entirely unable to identify a key compound. For two weeks, something was, shall we say, slipping through their fingers, eluding their eyes. The enigmatic compound was playing cat-and-mouse with them . . .

The scientist, it could be said, longed for the old days when he collected data on live animals with wires tapping their live brains. He had left the open brains, the wires, the dials, everything to his assistants. He now regarded with envy the weekly reports he received on those experiments.

Almost ready to abandon all this insanity of chemistry

tests, the insanity of feeding leaves or leaf distillates to people tempted him—certainly more enjoyable than lab work. Was he beginning to feel tired?

That evening, after he sank into his armchair and lulled his cat to sleep on his lap, he took the library director's most recent letter out of his shirt pocket and began to read.

It was already too late.

As he read the letter, a wave of anxiety swept through his whole being; he had experienced a similar sensation with the previous letter (although he wasn't certain that the letter itself had caused the anxiety). Now he felt close to defining the sensation. He knew it was entirely pointless to feel remorse for not having read the entire letter, or, worse, to search for the letter (he vaguely remembered tearing it up and throwing in the trash). Why on earth had he chanced upon this library director!

"I was both expecting and not expecting a reply to my letter," began the director. "You must have been angry." The words that were supposed to anger him must have been in the part he hadn't read. What could he have written? "This time, I will ask plainly: Do you also secretly grow tulips? You don't have to hide it from me. I do, and that's why I was appointed to this tiny, faraway city; perhaps I should say 'banished,' as rumor calls it . . . I have no misgivings about telling you. We can understand each other. When I started combing through the books to find information on the red-salamander, I was only thinking of providing a service beyond the borders of this tiny city. I had sensed nothing whatsoever. But when the eleventh-century manuscript described the red-salamander as *a plant closely resembling the tulip,* thoughts began stirring in my mind. What led those stirrings to their natural conclusion was both your veiled answer to my question in my first letter and your unwillingness to respond to my second letter. It's one thing to hear that other tulip growers

exist, but to be able to actually meet a real person who carries this passion in his heart would be something else altogether. . . . I beseech you, please do not leave me alone,
isolated . . ."

What a tangled mess!

He got up, laid his cat on his desk and, taking a blank
sheet of paper, began to write.

While weighing his words one by one, he caressed the
soft, warm belly of his cat, underneath its chin, its neck;
the undulant purring of the animal helped him forget his
fatigue and find consolation. (He considered asking the
library director whether or not he had a cat, but then
changed his mind). He finished the letter and put it in the
envelope; he carried his cat and laid it at the foot of his
bed; he undressed, washed up, pulled back the blankets,
and lay down.

2.

He was glad he hadn't responded to the second letter. The
small city was not small at all. From where he stood, he
could see two old structures, both obviously renovated.
Nor did he notice any dilapidated structures, at least for
now. The streets were paved. It must have rained the night
before; the place glistened in every direction. He asked for
the library, and found it two streets away, without difficulty. But about this building, he wasn't mistaken. Here
was the old wall and here the new—and freshly painted—
iron fence. He asked for the director at the door and was
shown to a room on the right side of the courtyard. Entering, he introduced himself and watched with interest the
expression of surprise on the director's face slowly turn
into unbearable, helpless astonishment.

He had traveled in the morning and was planning to
sleep in his own bed tonight. He just needed to speak with
the director, perhaps browse through the book, nothing
more; it would be nicer to skip the restaurants, the meals

with drinks and crowds! If they could just spend a few hours . . . and then, God willing, on his next visit, that time . . . The director's eyes assumed a cheerful glow, which meant that his invitation to "dine with so and so at the grand restaurant" was just a display of good manners.

The director read to him the entire section on the red-salamander in the old book about exotic plants. The legend of the tulip field was included in the last section titled, "Beliefs and Hypotheses Concerning Plants." The director showed him a few other books. One contained the phrase, "sand-tulip also known as red-salamander." Another stated, "the red-salamander, known for its medicinal use against itches, like the tulip . . ." And yet another treated the red-salamander not as a plant but as an alchemical term referring to the red vapor produced during the distillation of potassium nitrate; the same book also stated that thinking of the red-salamander as a plant—all thanks to a fairy tale—was a ridiculous misunderstanding.

The director had copied all these passages and sent them to him. (The unread portion of the second letter . . . And how much information he had been able to cram in there, this young man with the lovely face! How could he tell him that he hadn't finished reading his letter, that what the director perceived as an evasive response to his first letter was, in all honesty, due to the scientist's unwillingness to divulge any information on the effects of the red-salamander leaves? He decided: he would never tell him any of this.)

After they finished reviewing the books, the director invited him to his house. This was the real purpose behind the scientist's trip. Both men had impatiently awaited the opportune hour when they could leave the library and go to the director's house.

There was no cat in the house. Only a partridge in a wooden cage adorned with brass hobnails. The director held the scientist's hand and—as if reading the other's mind or as if he had read the letter that was never sent—took him to the solarium behind the house. Inside, there were fifteen or twenty pots with tulip blossoms of all colors, erect in their splendor. The solarium was surrounded by horse-chestnut trees that, in turn, were surrounded by tall garden walls. The director was watching the scientist's face without saying anything.The scientist's reaction must not have been satisfying enough: the two men did not stay here very long, and returned to the living room instead.

The partridge was pecking at the wood.

• • •

The host asked what he would like to drink. "Tea," said the scientist. Preparing tea would keep the host away, at least for a few minutes. He needed a little time to think. Not that he had anything to hide, but he wasn't sure whether he could trust this man. He walked and stood in front of the partridge. Whispering, he said something that made the bird happy; it pecked and cooed with ever more delight. When the host returned, the scientist had made up his mind. They sat facing each other; the scientist started talking.

He, too, had an interest in flowers. And like most others, he liked roses. Yet, while everybody else grew red, pink, white, yellow, this or that color roses, he was passionate about the green rose. Although it was called green rose, its true color was something between jade and turquoise. People who tried to cultivate it were both ridiculed and pitied; the director, too, ought to know that once you cultivated a blossom in this color, you had to start all over, grafting, crossbreeding who-knows-what-color rose with who-knows-what-other-color rose. A green rose could not be bred from a green rose.

The host listened with feigned interest, simply allowing an occasional, flat, cold "yes" or "of course" to show that he believed none of this talk. The scientist couldn't even convince children with this talk. He was giving himself away. Two or three lines written to the authorities would suffice. The host would show this know-it-all who was treating him like a gullible oaf what the world was really made of. He wouldn't let him off the hook by simply saying, "I'm not fooled by your game."

• • •

The host asked what he would like to drink. "Tea," said the scientist. Preparing tea would keep the host away, at least for a few minutes. Would he trust this man? He had to decide. He stood in front of the partridge. Whispering, he said something. The pecking stopped, as if cut off by a knife. He could hear the sounds coming from the kitchen—the teapot being set on the stove, water simmering, a jar opening, spoons and cups being set on the tray. When the host returned, the scientist had made up his mind. They sat facing each other. The host started talking.

"I wanted to show you my tulips first. So that you won't distrust me."

"I have nothing against tulips, but I don't grow them. That's what I wanted to write but thought that you wouldn't be convinced. And that's why I traveled here. Actually, I grow blue roses. You know, the blue rose . . ."

The host appeared to listen with interest. He was angry. If the scientist was telling the truth, then the young director had made a foolish mistake by giving himself away. If he was lying, then it meant that the host had failed to gain the scientist's trust. The rage brewing inside his isolation showed him the most primal path to revenge, as he sat and appeared to listen with interest.

• • •

The host asked what he would like to drink. The partridge suddenly stopped pecking. "Would it be alright if we didn't drink anything?" the scientist asked. "Don't trouble yourself. It would be better if we sat and talked instead."

It was obvious that the scientist wanted to hide something, the host thought. Instead of writing a letter, he was coming all the way here, mumbling something or another, showing no interest in his tulips—certainly not the kind of interest that they deserved, he had hoped at the least for that—starting the conversation in a hurry, chattering about blue roses. The host interrupted, "It is said that the blue rose aficionados consider it great mastery to grow the blue rose alongside a tulip, inside the same pot. What is your opinion?"

"I don't know," the scientist said, "I never tried, but I would imagine that growing the two together inside the same pot would be difficult indeed . . ."

The partridge resumed its pecking. As if it wished to break the silence and draw their attention to itself. The host whispered something to the partridge. The bird responded cheerfully. And the two men remained silent as if listening to the bird, but they were struggling, as if in a swamp. And each was aware of the other's struggle.

Standing at the door, his face partially illuminated by the light streaming from inside, the library director appeared entirely young, entirely childlike. What made him appear childlike was actually something other than his youth: a hurt feeling that had gathered, deepened along his lips and chin . . .

The scientist was sad. He didn't mean to hurt the director. Besides, he hadn't said anything hurtful. Yet the director was clearly hurt—like every person who imagines something and discovers that it amounts to nothing. True, the scientist himself had made a mess of what he had come here to explain . . . He looked at the director as sweetly as he could. "One day I will tell you, rather, I will *be able to* tell you how much I am indebted to you . . . Please forgive me, I don't like to talk about unfinished tasks." He paused than added, "Besides, it's not necessary."

The host tried to smile, as if he wanted to believe, but he couldn't. The hurt expression disappeared only briefly. Returning, it settled in the lower part of his face. Yet this time, it seemed more ambivalent, less childlike . . . The director's face now appeared quite beautiful. "Goodbye. Thank you very much. We will invite you to our laboratory, to thank you in front of everybody. I hope the day will arrive soon . . ." They shook hands. The director was trying to smile. Did the scientist trust him, after all? They waved at each other until the car turned the corner.

The scientist explained to himself the reason why the eleventh-century manuscript was more important than the thirteenth-century one, and he was convinced that his proofs were philosophically and logically sound, while all along he continued to wonder whether or not he was deceiving himself . . .

• • •

The director was angry with himself. Preoccupied with the tulips, he had failed to inquire about the red-salamander enough. Yet, the scientist's thankfulness had to do with that matter first and foremost. He had made a big mistake, and was back to square one, wherever square one happened to be . . . With myriad new questions swarming his mind . . . He would never learn.

Anticipating that he would be asked about the scientist's visit, he tried to invent a credible narrative that he could repeat with consistency. Once his heart was satisfied by his invention, he went to bed. The scientist also would soon be arriving home. They would see each other again.

Hadn't the scientist said so? The director would appear before him as an entirely different person. Repeating to himself the promise that it would be so, he fell asleep.

That evening before going to bed, the scientist gathered, folded and put away his travel-weariness, the anxiety gnawing at his heart, and the disquietude he felt at the expression of disbelief on the director's face. Whatever the outcome, he had to put this business behind him now. Besides, there was no sense in feeling sad. He imagined the look of surprise on the director's face when he thanked him in front of everybody. He smiled. Lifting his cat from his shoulder, he put it at the foot of his bed, and lay down.

3.

The climax in the red-salamander project arrived when the researchers succeeded in getting the plant to reproduce in the laboratory. They had good reason to be proud, no one could argue! This unknown, unfamiliar, vulnerable plant had come to like its new environment and was reproducing. The scientist and his assistants observed the plant through glass. One morning, all of them must have noticed the same thing since they turned to look at one another and stood motionless for quite a while. There was a bed of tulips before them.

They probably felt no need to voice their thoughts. Either the plant had experienced inconspicuous changes in this environment and was beginning to resemble the tulip, or there had been a resemblance from the start which they had overlooked—because of the plant's other, more unique properties—and which became, all of a sudden, obvious to eyes now familiar with the plant. Secrecy became more imperative than ever. Quite simply, tulips were being cultivated inside an official, state laboratory. Any outsider would say so.

• • •

So far they had been able to isolate positively a compound that they named *Aa*. While busy analyzing its structure, they were also attempting experiments to investigate the property that caused truthfulness—or more precisely, as the book described it, the property that "disabled lying."

Right about this time and quite suddenly, a rumor began spreading in every direction. One that was a hundred times, a thousand times bigger than any rumor that could have been started by a library director who refused to forgive being abandoned in his isolation.

He was surprised. The project had to move faster. Although he felt sad, he did not try to find the source of the rumor.

His friends who visited him always lowered their voices slightly when they began to say, "The other day . . ." The first time he heard "The other day," the story went on, "at a gathering, the conversation wandered around to the topic of flowers. Somebody said that you were growing tulips. I was about to say, I know him, he wouldn't grow tulips; I felt it my duty to say so, even though I knew that my objecting would only reinforce his opinion. But before I could open my mouth, someone else jumped in and said, 'Yes, it's true, and side by side with roses, in the same pot . . .' And the one who'd said this was a mutual acquaintance of ours. Honestly, even if forty people had told me that he had something against you, I wouldn't have believed it! How could he talk like this? I won't even look at him again . . ." The scientist had tried to calm his friend. It was common knowledge that their mutual acquaintance himself had grown tulips at one time. He couldn't have been malicious. Especially since he'd come to perceive growing tulips as an act of courage. "Who knows, perhaps he sees me as a man of great courage; perhaps he truly wants to believe that I am growing tulips . . ." Still, it was all a sad affair.

Afterwards, many of his friends brought him the same

news, each starting with the same "the other day." Some
had heard the rumors on the street, on the bus, and each
account deepened the scientist's sadness.

In the meantime, the lab work picked up speed. In all
likelihood, the book's claims would come true. The experiments were conducted with the tiniest possible sam-
ples: closely scrutinizing every step of the process, the
researchers experimented on dosages as small as one percent of the various compounds that would enter the
bloodstream of someone who ate a leaf.

Finally one day all the active ingredients were identified, and the dynamics of "inability to lie" was roughly
deduced. When *Aa* was not used, the effect of the limited
experiments lasted only for a few seconds. (The experimental subjects were asked outright to say something that
they knew was a lie.) But once *Aa* was added, the outcome
changed considerably, and when the dosage was increased
to five percent, the subjects, no matter how hard they
toiled and tried, remained unable to lie for hours, and in
certain cases, for an entire day.

These studies afforded the scientist a brand new out-
let, and he experienced a childlike joy. The day had come
to invite the library director and thank him in front of
everyone. Yet the rumors still continued, as well as his sadness about them.

Most importantly, the rumors had nothing in common
with the work being done in the laboratory, or, at least, so
it seemed to him; it appeared unlikely that any leaks regarding the experiments had been misunderstood or deliberately distorted. Word kept traveling from mouth to
mouth but always amounted to the same allegation: that
the scientist had a secret passion for tulips and was growing them in his home. At least, that was the extent of the
reports by his friends who told him: "Forgive us; we know
that you wouldn't want anything to do with us if you ever
discovered that we'd been hearing the rumors but keeping

them from you—that's why we bring you this sordid news."

• • •

The meeting seemed to go quite well. In attendance were the lab assistants, the heads of two or three relevant departments, a few high-ranking—very high-ranking—national security officers, and the library director. The scientist summarized his studies—of course saying nothing definitive, offering no real information—and thanked the director for his crucial role in the early stages of research. As he'd anticipated, he found delight in watching his face—this most youthful, most beautiful and, in the aura of this auspicious gathering, slightly frightened face—assume a look of amazement. He ushered the guests to the hothouse in which the red-salamander was cultivated, and described at length the delicate nature and particular properties of the plant that so much resembled the tulip. Afterwards, he invited the library director to his house; he asked him to spend the night, took him around the rooms, showed him his books, and his green roses. That evening, his cat did something it had never done before; it climbed on to the director's lap, curled up and fell asleep. As much as he wanted to say how significant his cat's behavior was, he didn't. The director might have found his words laughable.

In the morning, before leaving, the director said, "I guess a cat is a different companion from a partridge." To which the scientist replied: "To tell you the truth, I can't decide whether the cat shares one's solitude, or makes solitude more bearable." They took leave of each other. The scientist wondered if he would ever know the effect of the twenty-percent dosage he had mixed in to the director's coffee.

Three days later, he received an official letter from the mayor, bearing the stamp, "Top Secret." Referring to "certain information obtained" about his accomplishment—the amazing crossbreeding of tulip and rose—the letter asked him to sell a sample to the Municipality for purposes of cultivation in a special section of the Municipal Botanical Museum; and it requested the utmost confidentiality, indicating that this section would remain closed to visitors.

This time the scientist was quite confused and couldn't decide what to do. He weighed his options throughout the day, throughout the night. Even if he spent a lifetime trying, he would never be able to explain the truth to anyone . . . What if he were to mix a hundred-percent dosage in everyone's food, in everyone's drink. . . . An experiment of such magnitude would most satisfactorily demonstrate its outcome. Besides, he would have done everyone a favor. But he was the first to be terrified by the insane thought. "What has become of me that I can entertain such ideas. . . ." All this might be fine and good, but wasn't it certain that the leaf distillate (once its true effect was discovered) would be taken out of his hands, and used for all kinds of purposes, in the name of the State as well as of various private interests? Wouldn't his discovery lead to shady and dangerous practices? It would have been possible to destroy the plants, put an end to secrecy, and explain everything to the newspapers. Despite the troubles he would endure, it could be done. But to destroy all the lab records—to make everyone forget all the procedures— that seemed impossible. The letter from the Municipality led him to an unexpected awakening: the distillate he had mixed in the director's coffee, in a way, amounted to taking revenge on that innocent man. But what was the object of revenge? And whose revenge was this?

• • •

Thirty hours had passed since receiving the letter from the mayor. He was determined to keep separate the red-salamander and the tulip (rose-tulip or tulip-rose). Since he couldn't squelch the rumors, he decided to make them come true. He would contact his acquaintance who had once grown tulips, the one who was among the first to lend credence to the rumors; he would ask him for some tulip bulbs, or at least where he could find some. The bulbs used for medicinal purposes would not work. He wanted to find the finest blossoming variety. But even as he started his car, he changed his mind: there was only one place he needed to go.

He arrived in the small town when it was getting dark. He found the director at home: There was little surprise this time in his youthful, lovely face—which looked neither vulnerable nor childlike anymore. The partridge was again pecking. He noticed a small furry bundle curled up in a corner of the armchair that he was about to sit in. He looked at the director, then at the kitten. The man was smiling. "I'm not about to get rid of the partridge, of course . . . I am hoping that they will get used to each other. . . ." The scientist put the furry bundle on his lap. The kitten didn't even wake up.

He explained why he'd come. The director still showed no surprise. "To those who ask, I have been saying quite openly that I am growing tulips, and that your favorite flower is the blue rose, that you are cultivating the legendary red-salamander in your laboratory, and that you have nothing to do with tulips. . . . People who've known about our correspondence can't stop wondering, it seems. There are still others . . . You wouldn't believe . . . People who don't even know you, people who'd no idea that I've been growing tulips: they insist that you're growing the rose-tulip or the tulip-rose, as if they've seen it with their own eyes. Or rather, they used to insist. Ever since I went public, their curiosity has died out. But now they want everyone to know that they've no desire to

speak with me, that they avoid being around me . . .
What can I do? So I have a cat from now on . . . But,
tell me, why would you need tulip bulbs?

"Rose-tulip, tulip-rose, whatever its name, I've decided to grow it . . ."

Now the director did show some surprise. "I can give
you as many bulbs as you wish," he said. "When you grow
it will you show me?" Then he remained silent for a little
while. "Would you like to spend the night?" He didn't expect the scientist to accept the invitation. But he did. The
lovely face beamed cheerfully.

Early in the afternoon, he planted the bulbs inside the
rose—the green-rose—pots. He wrote a "Top Secret" letter to the mayor, informing him that he hoped to deliver
the requested order in six months at the latest. From now
on, he would be spending a few hours every day sitting
among the flowerpots, observing, experimenting. Waiting.
As if for death.

• • •

Thirty hours had passed since receiving the letter from the
mayor. In his "Top Secret" response, he indicated that the
information conveyed to the Municipality was false, that he
was interested strictly in blue roses; however, he added,
should the Municipality wish to assume the responsibility
of procuring the bulbs, he would, as a scientist (even
though such an undertaking remained outside his area of
expertise), attempt the experiments in his laboratory; even
then, he made sure to point out, the studies currently under
way in his laboratory made such a new project impossible
for the time being. Nevertheless, he offered to assist in es-
tablishing the specific ambient factors necessary for raising
in the Botanical Museum the tulip-like rarer-than-rare
plant called the red-salamander, currently being cultivated
in the laboratory for use in certain experiments.

Yet merely sending the letter would not settle the matter. The library director had to be persuaded to write an article about the ancient manuscripts; the article had to be published in one of those obscure scientific journals that no one read, and then, the issue in which the article appeared had to be sent to a foolhardy newspaper reporter. An exaggerated account released in one of the tabloids (especially if the Municipality were also implicated in the story) would arouse quite a bit of curiosity and create a healthy dose of chaos. The danger only existed for those who attempted to eat two leaves . . . For the rest . . .

• • •

Thirty hours had passed since receiving the letter from the mayor.

He entered his laboratory. He asked his senior research assistant to get a red-salamander leaf. Everyone was surprised. But no one dared to contradict him. The leaf arrived. Before anybody could intervene, he rolled the leaf into a neat morsel and, shoving it in his mouth, he eagerly chewed and swallowed it. "I had to be the first to experiment," he said. He glanced at the two assistants who had been his boatmen and helped him find the plant; the three men exchanged smiles. He had talked a great deal with them about the effects of the leaf. Because of their official position, the two always told the truth to their supervisors. And when they wished to hide something from their peers, they easily kept it to themselves. Nevertheless, various experiments had confirmed the effect of the leaf the two men had consumed while on the boat. In truth, only the scientist and his senior assistant had conducted these experiments. It had never occurred to anyone else to consider the possibility that they had eaten the leaf.

He called the two boatmen to his side, and together with the senior assistant they moved to the experiment chamber. That was when he asked for a second leaf. His old boatmen instantly intervened.

It would be impossible to test this second leaf on any volunteer; nor could it be tested on animals, if the objective was to obtain reliable results and validate the particular claims found in the book. The only remaining option was for the scientist to test it himself. Besides, the book did not specify the type of madness, and for a scientist, becoming a casualty of scientific research is no different from any work-related accident. This way, either the scientist would prove himself right and provide clear direction for future research, or the entire adventure could be dismissed at once and for all. He would enter the chamber with no mask, no protective suit, walk to the red-salamanders, eat a few of the leaves, and the matter would be settled. Besides, he could eat a second leaf anytime he cared to; it wouldn't be difficult. What mattered was to conduct the experiment when his assistants were with him.

These last words worried one of the assistants in charge of guarding the scientist. The scientist was speaking his mind, and it would be quite difficult to hold him back—they would have to tie him down with a rope . . . And doing anything like that would . . . "After you, then," the assistant said. "We will stay right by your side."

The scientist stated that unless a third leaf was brought to him, he would not eat the second one. This was the crucial moment and the assistant suddenly realized what was going to happen. The others were probably observing the situation exclusively from within the framework of the experiment, and not considering the necessity that after the second leaf, a third leaf must be eaten as well . . .

But the assistant . . .

He approached the scientist and whispered, "Why?"

The scientist merely squeezed his wrist.

He ate the second leaf. All three assistants now stared

at him, while the scientist gazed from one assistant to the other.

Madness arrived in the guise of a horrible pain. Half an hour after he ate the second leaf . . . He was straining not to scream, clenching his jaws. He began tossing around on the floor. Writhing with pain, every fiber of his body wanted to scream. "The animals would not have been able to express this," he tried to whisper. "It's as if my body is being torn apart." Then, his eyes open wide, he began to let out deep guttural sounds and then was beating his head against the wall. Suddenly, the scientist calmed down and said, "I am hungry," in a soft voice. He snatched the third leaf from the assistant's hand. Ten minutes later, the news spread from room to room, from the laboratory to the officials, from there to the media, the radio, the television: "Esteemed scientist . . . as a result of an experiment . . . high doses . . . dead. . . ." The bearer of the news, the one who penned it, was the senior assistant who had not eaten any leaves. As for the man who'd guarded the scientist, he was quietly smoking a cigarette.

The guard was thinking: I've never seen a smiling corpse until today.

• • •

Thirty hours had passed since receiving the letter from the mayor.

He drafted an invitation on a piece of paper and asked the guard to kindly take it to the printer. He had to stand watch by the machine. Exactly thirty-eight of them had to be printed. Twelve would include the phrase "with your spouse," the rest would be issued singly. The invitations were sent to the mayor, to the officials from previous meetings, to a few of his friends, and to the people whom he knew had been active in spreading the tulip rumors.

Standing at the door of the house, the guard carefully examined each invitation, and after the fiftieth guest, he closed the door. He was amazed that all the invitees had arrived. A few people always fail to attend these functions. Evidently, everyone had been sufficiently enticed by the rose-tulip or tulip-rose rumors.

In a matter of thirty minutes, the drinks prepared with leaf distillates of one hundred percent must have produced the intended effects: all the guests were talking without even noticing that they were saying things they would normally never have said. Before very long, the door began opening and closing furiously; the guests left one after another. After the last guest slammed out, the scientist thought that the air in the room was so thick with rage that you could almost smell it. He looked at the guard and smiled. "Good thing that this stuff has no taste," he said. "Let's call it a form of revenge, if you like . . . All my life, I tried not to lie. But you have to admit, don't you, that the first significant lie I decided to tell turned out to be the most beautiful one: it negated itself. . . ." He filled a tall glass and drank slowly. This was his first drink.

He was caught in dreams. Tomorrow he would write a letter to all the guests and explain everything. He would tell them that they were serving science. Fifty people would no longer be able to lie. But how many more, how many more people would have to be lured across his threshold so he could secretly serve them the leaf distillate . . . The end of all lies: wasn't that what he wanted?

1969/1972/1975

11.

fainted / dead / inaseaofpurple /
eyesshut / speechless /
gamenotoverisaid / charging /
thegreenvizierwasmine / tookhim /
almost / facetoface /
gamenotovergamenotovernotover

*O*pening my eyes, no one had moved; I tried to get up, and the hand I leaned on hurt badly; the small cleaver was covered with blood, and so was my costume. I was able to get up with the help of my other hand. I was standing among the objects I had dropped. I picked up my spear. I no longer looked at the mayor. He was announcing the Greens' victory with words petrified, centuries old. Beyond the trees, the jets in the pool came to life, boisterous water gushing up toward the sky. The Greens moved toward the water, and the Purples retreated without even looking at me. I felt deserted.

When I raised my head, I came eye to eye with a spectator a few steps in front of me. "Your move was supposed to be the one after the next," he said. "After defending his endangered men, the mayor was going to move you next and win the game. How could you have failed to see that moving prematurely meant defeat?"

The one standing next to him said, "The mayor controls the Purples, their players cannot see the entire game. They can't even budge. . . . But you, how could you fail to see that your insubordination is a fatal crime?"

They walked off, still discussing it between themselves. I remained in my place, squatted, laid my head on my knees. Then I raised my head, removed the handkerchief I had tucked in my purse, and wrapped it tightly around my hand. The bleeding would stop somehow, sooner or later. I laid my head on my knees again.

I was hungry, thirsty. I was cold. I didn't move.

ANOTHER PEAK

To İsmet Takgöz and Tarık Gülmen

Getting here had not been easy.

First he had to cross a plain stretching as far as the eye could see.

Over the years, he'd heard various stories about the plain and listened to them all with a mocking smile playing at the corner of his lips. They talked and talked and talked, weaving improbable stories. Some meant to frighten him, hoping that he would change his mind, as they spoke all those incredible words, now laughable, now lament-filled.

In all fairness, some storytellers had gone to the plain, and some had even attempted to cross it. Not everyone was telling a secondhand story, embellishing an account that grew a thousandfold after each retelling. There were indeed some who'd attempted the feat. But attempting was not the same as accomplishing. So how could he have wiped that mocking smile off his lips while listening to their claims?

Parts of the plain were covered with reed beds, and the

soil beneath these reeds was neither completely firm nor completely wet. But couldn't you walk around the reed beds without having to venture in? The longer route would probably be safer and of course you could. In fact, you had to walk around, but the path still wouldn't be much safer. Because in some parts of the path, as soon as you stepped on to apparently dry, parched soil, you found yourself knee-deep in mud. By the time you figured out where to set your foot down, and how to recognize firm ground, night fell. In the darkness, strange creatures came out of the reeds. Some were predatory, some knocked you to the ground. Some crawled, others swarmed. You were completely exposed on all sides; and even if you survived the night—even if not a single insect touched your body—you didn't have the strength to get up and walk in the morning. The night's humidity inside the dark reed bed, the ever-deepening venom of its rotting life, made you stiffer than a stone.

But let's say you did get up and walk. Could you spend another night, two, three more nights like this without getting anywhere?

These were the stories told by those who had returned after the first night.

They always described the dangers to your flesh, to your bones, and the silences between their words were meant to summon all the risks that would gnaw away at your heart and mind—the way despair, fears, worries always do. After all, none who'd tried it lacked courage; but the frailty of the flesh and bones had disheartened them. And for some reason, their courage, as much as they tried to make you feel it within each of the silences, had a way of disappearing in the course of the narratives.

He had listened many times. Still, he left for the road. On the edge of the plain, he took a deep breath and looked back at his village vanishing in the morning mist: then he entered the plain through the clearing between the first two reed beds.

Everyone had mentioned these first two reed beds. It seemed common knowledge that this clearing was the only entrance to the plain, and he did not look for an alternate route. If this was the known passage, why shouldn't he benefit from the knowledge?

After walking for an hour, he experienced his first surprise when he came upon a few men cutting reeds. Wasn't the plain supposed to be inhabitable, deserted, and so on and so forth?

He exchanged greetings with the men then continued on his way, feeling their gaze at his back. This was only the beginning of the journey; but still, his chest swelled up with pride.

He quickly came to expect the unexpected: He saw horses wandering aimlessly; frog-like creatures gurgling in the sloughs; and a wildcat darting out of a thicket, chasing an animal that resembled a rabbit. He plunged into the thicket, stomped through, and drank the water that, clean though it was, left a mold-like taste in his mouth; he walked alongside the stream, thinking this had to be the correct way to advance. He reached the head of the stream, but there was neither water nor vegetation any more.

He did not encounter other human beings besides those cutting reeds, but he didn't come upon anything truly dangerous either.

He spent the first night and each following night crouching beside a few large rocks he found here and there, and when he sensed a creature approaching him, he turned on his flashlight, trying first to see it, then to chase it away. Perhaps there were creatures he couldn't sense, but none ever touched him. Getting up in the morning indeed proved difficult, yet he didn't feel numb with the night's venom, or as stiff as stone.

In the beginning, his sack had felt heavy on his back. True, it would have been foolish to attempt crossing the plain by car. Of course there were beasts of burden on this earth . . . But eventually, he'd decided that he'd rather carry his own weight and his sack than to worry about steering and protecting an animal, or having to venture into potentially dangerous grazing fields. Besides, his sack was getting lighter. He felt a little tired, but he also knew that he was approaching the place where he could rest.

Next morning he folded his emptied sack and tucked it under his belt. Once the mist lifted, he saw, at a little distance, the chimneys of a village, with smoke rising from them. He quickened his steps. For the first time, he wasn't paying attention to the ground beneath his feet, and by the time he realized he had walked into loose, shifting soil, it was already too late.

The first house had seemed to be right in front of him, in fact, so close that he'd thought he could stretch out his hand and touch it; yet many hours passed before he got there, exhausted from hunger and fear.

But even while struggling horribly through the loose soil, he was wondering how it was possible that this village—described in all the stories as the farthest point— was known both to the people who conceded never having reached it, and to the people who claimed that no one could ever get there. All of a sudden, he understood that while thinking he would reach a village at the end of his journey—and, better yet, the very village described to him in great detail—he had been spurred by a childish hope. Day after day, night after night, he'd become more and more convinced that the accounts were mostly lies, or, at the least, they were built on shaky, unreliable information, but still, he had never, even for a moment, questioned the existence of the village. Yet since nobody had ever seen it, this village could well have been pure fantasy.

Yet the village was in front of him.

Somehow he managed to get there. Knocking on the first door, he was joyfully received.

Those in the house appeared to know why he had come. They offered him food, made him drink *ayran*, and afterwards, prepared a bed for him to sleep in.

When he opened his eyes, he saw fifteen or twenty villagers huddled around his bed, waiting for him to wake up. He exchanged greetings with them, they inquired about his health and hearth, talked about the air, water, earth and fire. They had plenty of grass, plenty of fruits; the animals were well-fed, so were the humans. Autumn would last long this year, winter would arrive late. The villagers were elated to have a guest. Many had wanted to come, the villagers knew; still, no one ever did. The oldest man in the village, an elder with a crooked back but a youthful voice, was saying that, in all his life, he had seen only one person coming from the other side of the plain . . . Yet—

The elder stopped talking abruptly. The others—he couldn't tell whether out of respect or out of shyness—waited without making a peep. But the elder remained silent for a long time.

Everyone was waiting for him to say something, he somehow realized. As if whispering, he asked respectfully: "Did he manage to climb?"

That's when, quite suddenly, everyone took a deep breath. As if a wind blew through the room.

Staring at the floor, the elder said, "Actually I was very young; I don't know whether he climbed or not," adding, "but if he'd climbed, it would have been told and retold over the years. And in my turn, I would have passed it on. No, he must have changed his mind and turned back without climbing. Who knows how disappointed our villagers must have been. They never said a word about this man whom I remember seeing so well. Otherwise, I can't explain their silence, even now . . . He must have turned back . . ."

Then silence returned and lasted for a long time. Until a youngster asked, his muffled voice cracking with anticipation: "Will you?"

Then, "Yes," the man said, "I came to climb."

Afterwards, he rose to his feet, opened the door, and walked out. He lifted his head, proudly looked up and beheld the mountain. On his way here, it had appeared as nothing more than a moss-colored wall rising beyond the village, and because he'd deliberately lowered his eyes—but why should we hide it, he'd been exhausted and in no condition even to raise his eyelids, much less his head—he had not seen the peak. Now the mountain stood before him in all its splendor. The peak he intended to climb was still hidden in fog.

• • •

Getting here wasn't easy.

But I know that it will be even more difficult from here onward.

Not because the climb will take effort, which is to be expected, rather because it will know neither day nor night—only movement unbroken, indivisible by hours.

I shake every villager's hand, bidding farewell. This time, my sack is not heavy. When I stop to rest, I should find fruit or grass or tubers to eat, clean water to drink, that's what the villagers tell me.

True, after a point, they don't know the path either; they have not ascended the heights. But seen from here, the remote, yet-unclimbed parts appear dense with trees. At least until the part where the first strips of fog begin winding around the mountain. Winding: wandering; meandering. Winding: tangling one with another; becoming difficult to untangle. Winding: intertwining, becoming enwrapped, rapt. That's how I must think from now on.

This peak is among the highest points in the land. I know. Climbing it, reaching the peak has been a feat treasured up in the hearts of countless generations of hopeful men. I know. Because there is an ancient, very ancient legend, passed on from age to age, which claims that, once on the peak, you can see the entire land, its past and its future entire.

Perhaps there are yet higher points in this steepest region of the land. I don't know. But what is absolutely known, what is recorded in all the books, is this: No other view rivals the one seen from this peak.

What makes its height impressive is perhaps the plain below. It has to be. True, outside this region, the rest of the land is also quite flat. The books do not altogether agree on the figures, but as everybody knows, this mountain couldn't be considered truly high. As a matter of fact, if one were to follow its access path carefully, climbing it should be as easy as climbing a mound.

As I start my journey these are my thoughts. Perhaps they shall never be thought again. I quickly move away from the village, taking the somewhat steep path.

"Paths stretching like thread." It's a cliché, common to many languages. My mind gets stuck on it. Or it gets stuck in my mind. Like thread . . .

that children loved to play

rather, there were threads I used to love playing with as a child. They were nothing like paths. Would I, can I, say the same thing now?

You know the threads. Of the kind that is pulled off a spool and snapped

the thread of a spool snatched at the blink of an eye from a sewing box, a thread that runs like a brook, coils like a snake, assumes shapes as in writing . . .

You single out a filament, draw it out of the thread, then another, then another. The drawn-out filaments have been drawn out haphazardly, then they are cast aside, never again to be looked at. The last remaining filament— the last one for no reason—seems heavy with thoughts, as if bearing the memory of brooks, snakes, writings, then it starts wavering by itself, and then it twists suddenly and snarls itself into a ball-like thing. Then, this ball is squeezed between the fingers until it turns black, when it is discarded. It has fulfilled its purpose. Now another piece of thread must be pulled from a spool in that sewing box which is always picked up and tucked away, hidden, impossible to find.

Like that. Ascending this hill is something like that. That is what I am thinking while taking my first steps along the slope, losing sight of the village now left behind the trees. But if you ask me why, I couldn't explain.

An elusive thought, at least for now. Yet, later on, perhaps somewhere well ahead on my path, this association will clarify itself in my mind. That's what generally happens.

Besides, don't I have to fill my time with something? What other business do I have in ascending the peak, if not to think of everything I have learned up to this day, everything I have experienced up to this day, along with the things I will see on this path?

Or, ascending the peak is something like reading, learning. Learning, rising above one's station, elevating oneself . . .

How easy it is, sliding from one word to another, to boost the value of the task at hand.

Yet when one climbs or walks, submitting to the whim of the path—always remembering that the path is nothing more than (and should always be called) a trail winding now this way, now that way—the task is not merely climbing, rising with each step.

Just like everything else in life . . . Nothing one does is entirely separate from the previous deed; yet every next step is not always ahead of the previous step—that kind of thinking is valid on the plain, not here.

I stop, rest, then continue walking. I look around, toss

a berry in my mouth, break a fresh stem to suck its juice. I walk. Or rather, I continue walking.

I am thinking of the wheel.

How does the wheel move?

The longer the spokes extending from the hub, the longer the circumference. Time per cycle must measure longer accordingly. In succession, each point along the rim must make contact with the ground so we can say that the wheel is moving; and each cycle of movement concludes—does it not?—only when the first point makes contact with the ground again.

But by designating a first contact point, are we not giving a construct more truth-value than it deserves? This kind of linear explanation feels inadequate. At the most, it may explain how I crossed the plain and arrived at the foot of the mountain; yet, what I am doing now is something else, something else entirely. Both what I am doing and what I am searching for.

To understand what it is, I must free myself from the linear plane. When we were children, no one told us that the schoolbook definition of linear planes would, years later, come true, become real, in our lives; but if someone had, would we have believed it?

To escape the linear plane, what if I tried something like this: make the rim wider and extend the spokes at various angles from the hub. The first spoke meets the rim at one edge, the last one at the opposite edge, while the spokes in between are set slightly, very slightly off from one another so that only two spokes, diametrical opposites, extend to the same plane. This way, each plane is separate from but also co-exists with the others. Each signifies a different field of vision, separate from but also related to the others . . .

This is not a new idea, I know. Yet, in every age, in every land, at least one person must discover this idea anew, imagine it, voice it.

Should I feel happy because the entire adventure of humanity fits neatly along the spokes of a wheel? I feel a kind of happiness. The child who tossed in his mouth the black cherry he coveted, this child, too, used to feel this kind of happiness in the past. Even though he found the cherry sourer than he'd expected, more bitter than he'd hoped, and spat it out.

Below, the village houses look like tiny gray, off-white, off-yellow rectangles. On one side of each tiny rectangle, dark and thin lines of steam rise from the patchwork chimneys.

Inevitably, my steps greatly resemble one another. But by now, the wheel must have completed its first turn. I sense the slight elevation. But I still have many more turns before I reach the peak.

From here on (I can say 'from here on' because I have stopped) each turn of the wheel will take longer; true, my path is becoming steeper, but my spokes are growing longer, and so is the circumference of my rim.

What difference would it make here whether I think, shout, shriek or tell some story or another? No one is here to laugh at me and call me a lunatic for talking to myself.

Am I beginning to understand why it is so important to climb this mountain?

A while ago, I could see children quarreling just beyond the willows along the creek that flows behind the village; now they are not even vague specks of color flickering in the distance.

The quarrels are behind me.

No, no, I correct myself, I mustn't allow these mental lapses anymore: not behind me, *below* me. I must get used to terms of elevation.

I must climb. Because the wheel, or the spinning wheel—this image, fleeting though it is, is a shadow, a darkness in my mind—must turn.

I must turn, yet not as a spinning wheel. Rather, as a wheel. I must move forward. Whatever "moving forward" may mean. I mustn't be caught in a fixed axis.

Otherwise, what is the heart's great struggle worth?

It's laughable, but the heart's worth, the worth of this piece of flesh the size of a fist

> when their flint blades slashed the chests of their captives on altars atop the temples, when they offered to the sun the heart still pulsating between the lips of flame, the exalted Sun Warrior watched the rivers of blood slowly running, widening, down to the base of the tower

>> In the country named "the navel of the moon," the Sun Warrior called his people the revelers "in the land of the cranes"

was it known only to the Aztecs? did they alone know the heart's worth among all the people who have graced the face of the earth? Who else thought that only the human heart can satisfy the sun's hunger for veneration?

This heart, this unpretentious, steadfast heart, so easily overlooked in health, this heart that summons us to wage the fiercest battle when it begins to fail, this heart whose genius is an enigma . . . if it is meant to spin around itself, what would be the point of making this heart endure?

I know a sentence, even if it is beautiful—or better yet, even if it has been labored over so that it expresses its intended meaning fully—can never describe that struggle, that battle.

Fighting a disease is an act of defiance against an alien infiltrator. But a failing heart probably brings a person face to face with himself. Instead of overcoming the obstacle, he tries to get around it, in order to live. That's when animal defiance and human defiance become identical. When the heart is fighting this battle, being a spinning wheel would be something darkly depressing, shameful to accept.

One must turn as a wheel, and move forward.

Still, one never knows how to overcome obstacles ahead of time.

The subject of health, too, is below me now. The little tree whose leaf I plucked and chewed while thinking about the heart has long disappeared behind the curve. The body that has endured thus far will be able to endure the rest.

If I could rid myself of the habit of sorting everything, stacking one thing on top of the other, like food boxes . . . It's time now to learn that all things are *inside* one another. Haven't I climbed here in order to look at my surroundings?

Did they not try to frighten me into changing my mind about crossing the plain? And why did they wish to change my mind? Envy would be too simplistic an explanation. Now the plain—empty, smooth, vast, tame, thirsty—stretches below me like those sacred grounds waiting to become battlefields.

Battles, ancient battles, battles in ancient times, executed by steadfast armies advancing toward each other, intent on trampling and killing each other—though without lifting their feet too high off the ground—those ancient battles somehow always waged in dust bowls . . .

This, too, is an old image, left from a childhood game, arriving from a far-away darkness—an image taking shape inside a riddle spoken with a child's indecisive, crackling voice:

Beetle-crusher, beetle-crusher
Where on earth is the beetles' crusher?

Quite nonsensical, like all riddles. And like all of them, a ball of yarn made of dreams, tangling up as it unrolls.

Like threads, *Beetle-crusher, beetle-crusher* . . .

Or I can call it: the start of an ancient battle.

On the one side, a crowd. Without spears, shields, lances, slings, or stones.

The neighborhood children who—sooner or later—always get beaten up. But most of them don't realize this. Plenty of blowhards among them. They won't deign to use stones or slings, but not because they know of a better defense than stones and slings: it's out of pride. Yet, since they have attempted to fight on this plain

> actually they haven't attempted any such thing; I should remember that I am spurring them on to battle on this plain.

and therefore must carry spears and shields, they carry neither spears nor shields

The battalion in front of them is small, very small but orderly and dense. It resembles a giant insect—with countless legs underneath its hermetic shell of bulging shields, and an antennae-like mesh of spears above it. A multi-legged, castrated insect with numerous antennae. Having long forgotten how to copulate, it only knows how to wage war.

More or less . . . This, too, is an image like the neatly stacked-up food boxes.

A whisper rises from the disorderly crowd of children: *Beetle-crusher, beetle-crusher; where on earth is the beetles' crusher?*

The hands holding the shields and the spears tense up with rage; the defensive wall, the shell covering its body, remains perfectly intact, unmoving, but the shields and the spears do appear to quiver all at once.

Yet their spears are sticks, their shields, a few layers of newspaper held together with ropes.

I suppose the beetles are the unruly children. But why do they call the magnificent battalion in front of them "beetle-crusher"? How did this peculiar term manage to enter their vocabulary? They don't know, but they are able to infuriate their opponents by merely asking a question. And why are they so infuriated?

More or less . . . I suppose the fine distinctions that gain significance in mid-life become insignificant again later on. Later on, along the road, or somewhere along the climb . . .

Next, I imagine, the crowd of children with the blowhards—yet always the whipped—suddenly appears to have changed its mind about infuriating, taunting and defying the opponents, or at least, the crowd seems to have decided not to wait for the assault. As if by unanimous consent, the children slowly gather into an orderly group in front of the giant insect, the beetle-crusher battalion, which, while still ostentatious, now also appears to be a little anxious. The group begins to move as a single body, marching away, toward the other end of the plain. Utterly confounded, the beetle-crusher battalion watches the retreat of the children—the sole reason of its existence, its order, its magnificence, its suspense. What is left for creatures caught in such suspense? What is left?

Out of the neighborhood fights and riddles of our childhood, I have fashioned the onset of an ancient battle on this vast plain

it's not even the onset

why this mental association? can I explain it at least to myself? I don't know; but my imagination doesn't stop . . .

I ask myself what remains for these creatures caught in such suspense? At the most, an enormous inexplicable urge to make love. Like the waves of a boundless sea, rolling on top of each other, making love from one end— of the battalion, of the giant insect—to the other.

First, the insect will come undone, its antennae will fall, its shell will disintegrate. The helmets will tumble and roll about at its feet. All of a sudden, human forms will emerge. Young, strong humans suddenly awakening to the surge of lust that had been building inside them while they pressed their shields hard against their chests, and held their spears with rock-solid arms. Soon they will empty themselves out, lost in the swarm, the lovemaking that befits the majesty of the battlefield.

The other, slowly retreating crowd has already reached the remote peripheries of the plain, and will soon disappear from sight—wishing nothing else—without turning back, without trying to take advantage of the situation. On this ancient

> plain that couldn't even be a battlefield
> only the gratified and tired
> humans who give themselves to each other's embrace
> with the half-conquered coyness of first-time, adoles-
> cent lovemaking, and await sleep on beds made of
> shields, only those humans will remain

Yet, near the peak, even love seems to lose its significance. The land below is too far away now. Everywhere, yes, everything will soon lie entirely beneath my gaze. Until now, I've tried to convince myself that love can be experienced without lovemaking just so I could spare my life in the midst of this devastation, among the creatures that one could love but not make love to. Now, from this vantage point, it's much too easy to say, What's all the fuss about love, after all.

All the fine distinctions that hinge on imprecision—on more-or-less—will lose their significance from here onward. Beyond living more-or-less, there are countless other ways of living. Living as well as can be imagined. Besides this, what else is life?

Isn't it strange how we build a life? A piece of thread, a nail, a bottle cork, a piece of paper, a rag, a bit of dust, a few nothings . . . This ingathering is what we call "life."

For some time, I have been walking through the fog.

It's not by accident that my thoughts run along these lines. The fog, I know, means I am nearing the peak.

Yet this experience of nearness, doesn't it, too, seem to be losing its cherished place in my heart? Leave aside the early part of my journey, even when I started climbing the mountain, my whole being reeled with the immensity of my task. But now, as I am nearing the peak, about to conclude my ascent, what keeps me on my feet, what carries me forth is not the thought of reaching the peak. Perhaps because one feels pride when recognizing that the destination is near, that one has finally arrived. I have come along so far that I am above everyone. From here on, a little further up, I only need to pass through the fog and reach the peak, and once there, simply turn my head from side to side and see the past and the future of everything. The peak is the end. Wouldn't one ask: So what if you see? To whom can you describe all that you see, unless you descend? And descending, I suppose, is inconceivable. To this day, the books—however few—have described climbing up. But nowhere is there any mention of descending. If anyone ever carried down the knowledge he gained, it is not known.

Besides, he who arrives would not descend easily . . .

The idea of the spinning wheel returns as a piercing headache . . . From now on the only reason that compels me to reach the peak is that I have climbed this far . . . Nothing else. He who climbs so far does not return without reaching the peak. Returning now would undermine the value of human toil. Perhaps this is childish reasoning, a very flimsy excuse, but that's how it is . . .

Slowly, very slowly the fog recedes. If I take three more steps, I will be standing on the peak. I take the steps and I stand. First I turn and face the setting sun. I'm awed by what I see: my eyes, my heart, my mind must work together with utmost intensity, with intelligence gathered over an entire lifetime. I think: No matter what it takes, I will descend and explain to those below this awesome miracle as fully as my eyes and my heart and my mind have comprehended it. Slowly I turn around my own axis, certain that this is what I must do.

Without getting here, I never could have envisioned what I see from here, standing at this point, so far removed even from the thought I had three steps ago. Incomprehensible! No one ever attained this knowledge, this intelligence.

The setting sun gently warms my shoulders. I delay my descent. Dazed by the sun, my eyes can't see well, but with the light now behind me, I discern everything. Below me is the immense world, minuscule. Around me, far, very far below, thousands, tens of thousands of tiny, tiny objects arranged side by side by side: the world with its human beings, its fields, its workshops, its trees, its animals, its houses . . .

The man standing on the peak now stands above everything, with his intelligence, his majesty. The man on the peak looks into the distances, at the farthest spaces illuminated by the sun. . . .

He looks, the man on the peak, he looks, and looks, and sees, there, in the distance, another mountain. One much smaller than his mountain, to be sure, but still tall enough to be called a mountain. Something seems to be moving on top of that mountain, something like an insect, an animal . . . He stops, he freezes when he recognizes that the insect, the small animal-like thing, is a human being like him. He looks. He looks. He looks. There is a human being on the mountain facing the man on the mountain. Far away, very far away from him, and therefore very small, like an insect, a tiny animal. But straight before him. The other, too, turns and looks, it seems. The other, too, probably likens the man facing him to an insect, a tiny animal.

That's when he realizes why those who climb the mountain never descend. He sits, holds his head between his knees, and waits for darkness.

August-November 1972
January 1973

12.

The sky was turning dark. I removed all the metal gear on me, got up with difficulty and walked. Among the trees, a cat was sleeping on the grass under an oak. Perhaps it was the same cat. I tried to approach quietly. It didn't stir. I knelt beside it. It probably was the same cat.

I raised my head. He was standing in front of me, in white trousers, white sweater. The darkness of his tan complexion mixed with the crimson shadows of dusk. He sat down. The cat was still asleep. He was silent but I could easily read his mind.

You thought wrong.

Why?

I was already yours. But

I know. I was impatient, and lost the game,

I wasn't talking about the game.

It was a fatal crime, too, so said a spectator.

Until three hundred years ago, for committing that crime you'd be executed by the Greens' leader.

If one of you were to do it . . .

The Greens' leader still administers the punishment.

So now you will kill me.

That was until three hundred years ago.

And my punishment?

They've brought your belongings to the garden gate. You will leave town tonight and never return.

And you?

I'll come with you.

Where?

Where you go.

With me. . . .

With you.

But you . . .

You thought wrong.

You were not . . .

I wanted to mislead you, test you.

You must be a dream. That's why you say these things. The other day, here . . .

I haven't been in this garden for a week. Since the time when you sat at the table behind me and waited for me to turn and show you my face.

You are now in my dream, I said. I must become myself again, I must get up and leave. Have my hand bandaged, eat some food, sleep. You're now in my dream. Like water.

He did not speak. He fell silent suddenly. Or he spoke and I couldn't read his thoughts.

I raised my arms and laid them on his shoulders. I was squeezing my fists. I pressed my arms and gingerly pulled him toward me. He laid his head on my shoulder. I laid mine on his head. Again I could hear his thoughts. Tell me again and again, he said, tell me you love me, tell me you love me. We stood motionless for a few seconds that felt like hours. He softly tapped his head against my cheek, my ear, against my shoulder.

I could barely speak. "It's getting dark. Let's get going. Help me."

He held my healthy hand and pulled me up. The cat was still asleep.

We had only taken a few steps. He wrapped his arms around me with the pressure of twenty arms. Twenty arms at once crushing me, suffocating me. "You can live my life, you can make me live," I wanted to say. I couldn't.

The sidewalk was dark under the trees. A bright hole appeared in the distance. Standing on its edge, his dark face, his dark hands struggled to resist.

The hole grew dark, then closed.

WHERE THE TALE
ALSO RIPS SUDDENLY

For Yavuz and Patrick

L'amitie est avant tout certitude,
c'est ce qui la distinge de l'amour.
Elle est aussi respect, et acceptation
totale "d'un autre être."
—*M. Yourcenar,* Le Coup de Grace

1a.

Through 1968 and 1969, I had planned to organize these tales around the hours of the day. Past noon, the successive tales would, by the sixth hour when the sky inches its way toward darkness, change in tone and turn increasingly dark. But near midnight, the hope of a new day would seep into this darkness. In the foolish excitement of planning, I had decided that "even if many of the tales had no room for happiness or hope, the twelfth tale should bear traces of happiness, of hope." I had only one condition regarding this pact with myself: I would write the twelfth tale at a time when I felt happy, when I had taken leave from hopelessness and unhappiness. Yet, only a few of the tales ended up "less dark." How could I have made the rest "increasingly darker"? Furthermore, I speak of taking leave, but it never quite occurred over the years. Once or twice, I thought it did but in the blink of an eye I realized I was mistaken.

One time I experienced what I would call a "bloody" happiness. That's when I wrote not the twelfth but the thirteenth tale: The one that stood outside time, the tale that would function as the cradle for all the rest, and perhaps the one that most underscored the only form of happiness that can exist outside hope. . . . I'm trying to translate into human language the ripening process of a fruit, its release from immaturity, and I suspect I am prolonging too much its likely time span. Blame it on my being a circumspect tree. This is the best I can do.

Now this book has to end. I never think whether or not I am happy. In the past few years, I came to accept that what I have been searching for is not—could not be— "happiness"—regardless of how you define happiness . . . (Or we can settle the matter by calling "happiness" what we experience every time the tiniest hope is fulfilled.) In short, happiness perhaps means accepting unhappiness or hopelessness. [But *accepting* unhappiness or hopelessness depends, above all, on truly *learning* them . . . Recently, I met someone who taught me this (someone who believes in his own fabrications before anyone else will, someone who is quick to feel sadness when met with disbelief, or appears to be so).]

I can now write this tale, finish the book.

2a.

My first thought was something like this:

1b.

How I wish we were like cats. I have often felt like saying so. Cats seem fully aware of living in the present moment. If they are sitting by a hole and waiting for something, it is quite difficult to distract them. Say, there is something

happening somewhere they know well, something they
have watched every day and in which they've participated
in their own way (what we don't understand is that watching is itself a form of participating) they never hesitate to
get up from where they have been sleeping to go watch
. . . Whatever stage of sleep they are in, they experience
the sleep of that stage.

As for us, while we pride ourselves in having invented
chronology, while we perceive every task, every word as
being performed or uttered in order to reach a future
point along that continuum, we quickly dismiss the task or
the word at hand. Aimed toward a goal, caught in the
dream of a goal, we don't notice in the slightest the singu-
larity, the unchangeable and irreplaceable nature of every
moment in the string of moments that later—after our
death—will be called our life, and even more encompass-
ing, our *destiny*. (A few isolated memories of this life may
linger in the minds of one or two of our loved ones, but
the only person—our self—who can know that these
memories once belonged to a continuity, that they were
once meaningful, would have long perished in the vast
emptiness.) I said, "we don't notice," but let's suppose we
are truly near the end of our life. If I am not mistaken,
some of us (at that point on the road) do realize and learn
certain things: to remain quiet and to listen, for instance
. . . To feel, somewhere in their being, the weight of
everything they have done, seen, or heard. A child's laughter, sunlight seeping through, the roundness of a teardrop
inside one's palm, its soothing coolness, that it is innumer-
able, that it defies numbers altogether, or that happiness
might mean experiencing every sorrow, every joy, each
and each, impartially. And if one has grown old enough:
that the past experiences can return to aid and sustain
everything seen, heard or tasted. . . .

But we mustn't love the beloved the way we love cats.

2a.

My first thought was something like this:

"THE GREEN-EYED SCULPTURE"

The ancient tale of the Cypriot master who fell in love with his own sculpture has been told and retold over centuries, and even at times relived—as seen in the case of Buonarotti who screamed at his Moses, "Rise and walk!"

Yet this sculptor with the sweet gaze was modest. He made his statues neither of ivory nor marble. In other words, he did not sculpt. He used mud, he used clay. Consequently, he didn't consider himself a sculptor. He did not sculpt, he moulded.

For many years, the master with the sweet gaze could not find the clay he was looking for. He didn't bring ivory from distant lands across the sea like the Cypriot master, and he didn't search the marble quarries to find the finest slabs with the most distinctive veins like the Florentine master. He traveled, the artist with the sweet gaze. He traveled and looked for clay, weighed it, and began to work. Sometimes, if he found good clay, and after toiling liked the form he had moulded with his whole being, then he would set it on a high shelf to examine it for a while; he'd step closer, move away, try to correct the mistakes he found, and then examine it again.

[(*Later on, something careless would surely happen: either he or the housekeeper would topple the figure, breaking or bruising it. The artist would be sad, but before too long he would find even better quality clay, or at least he'd think he'd found something better, and begin the work anew. . .*)

I was going to turn this into a fairy tale; one day, I would make him discover a new layer of clay in the garden of his house, his atelier. He would mould this clay, marveling at the perfection of the form he finished, and wishing that it would come to life; the next morning, this clay figure would appear before him as a beautiful creature with green eyes. The artist would fall in love, but in due time, he'd realize that he could not make this living form respond to his heart's wishes, much less continue shaping it as much as his hands desired. Even parents appear ridiculous when they say, "I made you," never mind a sculptor who had fallen in love with his own creation, a clay figure that had come to life. But the day would arrive when the sculptor and the sculpture would learn to live together. The one would not seek his due for the sweat and toil he added to the clay from his garden, nor would the other wear as a crown the pride of having come alive. The sculpture would have sculpted the sculptor: he would have become an artwork made of materials finer than the finest stone: flesh, bone, and blood . . .

Frankly, such a miracle ending would have been heart-breaking, reversing altogether the scenario I'd been trying to work through in my mind. Turning both of them into "created creators" would have settled everything much too agreeably.]

1a.

In my whole life, I have experienced just one event, heard just one story that made the dreaminess, the optimism of fairy tales seem plausible. In fact, early on, when trying to imagine "the only happy tale," my initial idea was to compose a eulogy praising the people who had really lived through this "one story". . . But to put it in writing effortlessly . . . would have been both a lie and a disservice, a disservice to my friends who'd succeeded in creating that story. . . .

It wasn't accidental, the notion of arranging the tales starting with the noon hour. I often hear of writers who begin to write at the misty hour of dawn, writers who work in front of a window that always receives the morning light, the morning sun, whatever the season; I have even met a few of them. I envy them.

But the morning hours are my hours of struggle: I can do everything that forces me to be someone other than myself, but I have no desire even to write a letter any time before noon. Every morning I must adapt myself to the world, to people, to my surroundings. Even talking seems difficult—at least, talking without being quarrelsome, hurtful or disagreeable. . . As for writing—I've often said it—writing is not a means that I care to use for unleashing my anger, my pain. I can respect people who perceive writing as a means; yet when I first held a pencil, I decided that I would never pour out my raw pain, my raw anger— even if my writing bears *residues* of my pain and anger. My day begins after the noon hour, and continues—widening, ever widening—until the quiet hours of the night.

Yet books must also come to an end at some point.

1b.

We mustn't love the beloved the way we love cats.

But even though I recognize that loving this way is a mistake, I attempt, time and again, to experience what I call "cat love." A person can understand a great deal, but, in a sense, he doesn't learn. Or he doesn't learn to behave in accordance with his understanding. What causes him to commit the same mistakes again and again is a disposition, a "resolve," a "sense of destiny" he carries with him from his past, from his very distant past. Success becomes possible perhaps only if the framework of this disposition, this "resolve," this "sense of destiny" can be broken. How many times have I caught myself red-handed, sliding little by little into "cat love." Yet each time, I could come up with beguiling pronouncements, justifying to myself and to others that in these particular circumstances nothing else could be done . . . We are so fond of the easy path!

1a.

Books must come to an end at some point. That's the way it is for the writer. Whether he writes "from the heart" or not. (Of course, what "from the heart" means depends on the writer. Some want "to describe," some "to put into words," some "to teach," some "to invent." And who knows what else?) Arranging words upon words or (another image:) setting them together (another image:) in order to weave an original tapestry is not always an enjoyable task. Especially if one is not trying to put forth a theorem complete with its premises and conclusions . . .

1b.

To love a cat means to accept from the start its heedless independence in relation to the one who loves the cat (and whom the cat loves). It means to embrace—with a childlike sense of entitlement—the possibility of displaying, in turn, the same heedless independence. A cat snuggles next to you when it cares to; if it doesn't feel like snuggling, it leaves your appeals unanswered. After three or four strokes begins the purring, the gentle gurgling, which intensifies gradually; a bond has been established. But this bond can suddenly turn into a conflict if you've slightly moved and disturbed the cat's comfort or if it has reached sensory overstimulation. What has come to be known as a cat's "ingratitude" is this "selfishness"—a quality of human conduct ascribed, in turn, to animals. If we attempted to play with a six-month-old infant who possesses the willpower of an eighteen-year-old, the result would be exactly the same. . .

Responding to this selfishness with great patience and

love pleases our hearts, of course. To what extent the cat is aware of the meager happiness it affords us, I cannot tell, but the more meager the happiness, the more we are its slave. (Some people love a cat almost to the point of torture, I am not forgetting them. But excepting only those who hurt the animal—or the human being—in order to convince themselves of their strength, every cat-lover, even the most disciplined, knows this slavery.) Then one day, the cat decides to be affectionate, playful, coquettish, and we show weariness or indifference—imitating the cat. The cat is confused: whatever happened to the rules of the game, the rules we had agreed to from the start—that the cat would act like a cat, and the human being like a human being?

2a.

One story intrigued me for years. A story I had reread carefully in the narcotic stillness of the British Museum, bowing under the rigid rules of English bureaucracy . . . (Aldous Huxley was interested in the same story; it made him write an essay and liner notes for the jacket of a musical recording.)

1b.

Everything boils down to this: when we love a cat, we meet the animal's "selfishness" with our superior sense of forbearance and god-like mercy. Our insuperable greatness forgives every mistake, but also squelches the one committing those mistakes. Yet doesn't this exaltation, this invincible, god-like benevolence serve as armor for a person terrified of missing out on even the smallest crumb of love he receives or might receive and therefore is willing to accept everything (cruel or kind) from everyone—foremost from his loved ones? The person who suffers the nightmare of constantly trying not to hurt, offend or alienate people, the one who always perceives himself as their inferior? Seen from this angle, much becomes understandable: This type of love rests on imbalance, on a basic inequality . . . Yet we think or dream of love, anticipate it, always in terms of equality. Even when we upset this equality with selfish, monopolizing tendencies, aren't we perceiving our counterpart's every mistake because we believe in equality?

2ᴀ.

It is the story of a person born in the second half of the sixteenth century, one of the three or four figures whose art has been blowing like a wind across the centuries.

1b.

Perhaps the happiest tale is the one about the lovers who grow to respect each other, and experience—or try to experience—the miracle of genuine equality in love, even if they have to die and be buried in order to come together . . . The cardinal virtue worth learning is perhaps equality.

2ᴀ.

Yet while that man was wasting his life away between the poles of inequality, the world he shaped out of sounds was itself achieving equilibrium.

1ᴀ.

When I decided to write this tale, I wanted to keep in mind the example behind "The Green-Eyed Sculpture." An ivy-like, tenacious, smothering relationship between two people—one of them advanced in years, self-possessed, refined, blessed with the virtue of stillness, the other untamed, the rawest of the raw, one of those people who, we tend to think, are born with such beauty so to lend the world a purpose.

I had known the former for years—in a way I knew him well, in a way I didn't . . . The latter I knew only from a few lines in a few letters that referred to him as "the cat." Sometime later, or rather, many years later, I met him in person and learned the name he went by. The story of a relationship like theirs had to be written, I thought. But not in terms of common, everyday details or its chain of events—that's been written many times already. Yet I imagine people who know what a monumental achievement it is to sustain a relationship without damaging it or letting it rot from the inside, will appreciate the attempt to describe and praise this accomplishment. From the very beginning there was "the cat." And someone who loved "the cat." And I ask you this: an author who has had his share of successes in life, yet who has done nothing but move from failure to failure in what he considered one of his most important undertakings, why shouldn't he aspire to write a fairy tale?

2a.

The man born in the second half of the sixteenth century was noble by birth, but he quickly defied the codes and privileges of his class. As for his subsequent rise to that other elite circle, that seems—at first sight—to have been more a matter of destiny than of willpower.

2b.

A destiny which was first at work when he found his way into the arms of a twenty-year-old widow whose husband was rumored to have died of "excessive lovemaking," and later, when he reconciled—or seemed to be reconciled—with the young paramour his wife enjoyed for two years (after she was quite satisfied—or seemed quite satisfied—

with her new husband for their first two years together). And yet, his patience must have run out when he resorted to the age-old custom—practiced even today in his country—of cleansing his honor, and consequently his name, with blood. Like another musical composer.

2c.

Yet, something keeps simmering throughout this particular tale. Since such affairs never remain secret, especially in those days in his country, how did he manage to endure for two years all the nicknames and all the humiliation? Did he act as if he knew nothing—or everything? Did he act like he didn't care? Did he blame it on madness? Did he play the part of the proverbial husband who is always the last to know, or did he invent excuses—that vengeance was repulsive to him, or that he loved his wife so very dearly? Did he say, "The public's abuse is nothing compared to the savage wound I must bear inside"? Did he hide the fact that he thought or sensed or perhaps even knew that the newborn placed on his lap was not his? Or had he so racked his brain for months that the simplest of solutions assumed the cruelest resonance?

2b.

This much is known: Four years after the marriage, two years after being forced to share his wife with another man, he takes three servants, ambushes his wife and her lover, and orders them killed in their bed.

2c.

Why did he go into hiding for months in one of his mansions? We must consider the customs of his time: he is not being pursued for having committed a murder, and he is not hiding from the law. In fact, the murders were

overdue, long overdue! But he is running from his wife's
family, her lover's family, from their vengeance; because
only a noble can kill another noble. It is his right to kill his
wife and her lover, true, but he did not kill them with his
own hands; he ordered his servants to perform the deed,
and he didn't make a secret of this. In addition to violating
this custom of the nobility, he had also eliminated his second child (had his second child eliminated), the one he
didn't believe was his.

2b.

Four years after this episode, he remarries, moves to his
new wife's native city, and takes up residence in a mansion
inside the overlord's palace. The era of political difficulties
is over for the city; all necessary undertakings have been accomplished, ushering in the death of eminence. However,
in the twilight of this dusk also comes the burgeoning of
language and musical arts. Inside the modest houses on the
side streets of this city that displays the balanced splendor
of massive stone walls with fairytale gardens, inquisitive
minds from the remotest lands live and work together with
other elite artists from nearby. In an era bent on the pursuit
of new possibilities, new forms, new genres in language and
in sound, our man, too, will rise to prominence and become
one of the greatest new masters of music.

3a.

We casually say: "Artists' accomplishments are important,
not their personal lives."

2c.

In this century as in many centuries past, music is conscious of finding its origin in the human heart, the human
pulse, steps, throat, hands, feet. Even more constant than

the cogwheels and mainsprings of a clock, its measure is in the human soul, the human toil, the scientists' experiments . . .

3ᴀ.

In any case, that's how it seems from one particular angle. Yet, as far as certain artists are concerned, you can also find their personal lives, at least a few fragments of those lives, interspersed among their artistic works.

1ᴀ.

What did the older one bring into this relationship? The wisdom of his vast experience, the intelligence of desire and of the effort needed to fulfill one's desire . . . "The cat" had to be educated. Was educated. Besides, everything prior to the education of "the cat" remains outside this narrative. What matters is the education: the act of learning, the capacity to learn, remaining one's self while being molded, while learning the rules and regulations.

Years later "the cat" one day finally grew weary of the pressure. It was good that he had eagerly submitted to the pressure for all those years. And it was just as good that he finally grew weary of what he recognized as pressure. Under the circumstances, he could either pack up and leave, or he could pretend to remain faithful to the terms of the relationship while acting just as he pleased. At first he did the latter, ruining the labor, the mutual labor, of all those years. Afterwards he packed up and left. And afterwards he returned. With all his independence.

In the meantime, both men ended up learning the do's and don'ts, what was possible and what was not.

Works, great and small, are built by laying one stone at a time, day after day; death, too, is built like this, with a stone chisel that slowly loses its edge, day after day, night after night; death, great and small.

2c.

From here on, we can be a little inventive.

2b.

Gesualdo will die about nineteen years after entering the Ferrara palace as a bridegroom. Whether he stays in this palace or spends his time in one or a few of his countless mansions, he shuts himself off, shunning human company . . . As a father, he is ill-fated: the child who loves him dies and so does the child who cannot forget that he had ordered their mother's murder. There is also the rumor that one of his daughters "fell into a bad way."

2c.

We could say that his second marriage was not particularly successful either.

Yet we could also observe something uncommon about his life.

2b.

He always has a specially trained servant whose duty is to whip his master. According to his biographer, another renowned contemporary personality comments about the whipping—perhaps to be discreet (just perhaps)—in Latin: When he is not beaten, Gesualdo "*cacare non poterat*". . .

2c.

On account of the crime he commits in his youth, the crimes that follow afterwards, the man never enjoys peace in his life. It is heartbreaking that someone would have himself whipped—even if he does so by hiring a private servant—in order to atone for his crimes. But as much as it is heartbreaking, don't we think differently about his predilection when we learn (sinking to our century's pop-psychology level) that he cannot defecate unless he receives a whipping?

1a.

The respect the hunter must feel toward his prey has long been forgotten. The prey may or may not surrender to the hunter, but would the prey ever think of acting disrespectfully? The terms of their relationship would be violated from the start. A prey without respect, we might say, perceives itself not as the prey but as the hunter. Is the relationship merely reversed? I don't think so. I would say it is destroyed completely. We are left with two creatures that can think of nothing but crushing each other.

And this hunter-prey relationship has from the start been a recurrent theme—explicit or implicit—in fairy tales. I have thought a great deal about people who spend their lives believing that they are the hunters until they suddenly realize that there is no prey left to hunt and that they themselves have long ceased being hunters.

2c.

To what extent the whipping might have affected his music, I can't say. It is interesting to note, however, that this man who endured so much suffering and, still craving, hired a servant to inflict even more suffering (just as he had hired servants to commit the murder), composed short, playful, lighthearted pieces. And that he gave each sound its due and honored each equally; that he let no composition become predictable or rigid; that he refused to constrain the freedom of sounds; that he turned his back on everything that did not "move forward"—everything that looked back, everything that did not wish to forget the past.

1a.

One of the traditional eastern narrative forms (stories within stories, frames within frames) has preoccupied and tempted me for as long as I can remember. In this form, too, there is forward movement. But often a cyclical movement as well. Even when the form is not cyclical, its charm, its peculiar quality still satisfies the reader. There have also been some extreme examples of the form that thrusts the story forward while seemingly flashing back. Regardless of variations, the narrative form always appears headed toward the innermost story, the innermost frame. It intends to lead the reader to a core, a pip, if you will. Whether tasteless or inedible, a pip that one reaches by eating and eating into the flesh of the fruit, a pip that is the harbinger of the next tree . . . These stories, these frames, afford writing a modicum of freedom from linearity.

2c.

I wonder if there were not one or two love interests that remained secret in Gesualdo's heart, in his life story. Didn't the pain of mistreating love add to his pain?

3b.

In response, I will simply quote a statement I read some-where: "Moi seul, je sais ce que j'aurais pu faire . . . Pour les autres, je ne suis tout au plus qu'un peut-être." Doesn't this force us to acknowledge how empty and bar-ren and worthless is any desire to achieve equality between the lover and the loved, the gazer and the gazed, the hunter and the prey? Equality—yes, we still would like to think—will perhaps be achieved inside the reality of mu-tual inequality . . .

1a.

We seem entirely unamazed by our existence in this world, and that this existence actually persists. The tales result from my amazement about this indifference. Walls keep rising between the sick and the healthy, the guilty and the innocent, people in the minority and those in the majority. Always "they" are the ones building the wall, so we say, evading our responsibility. From which side is a wall built and why? The question is still valid . . . But some of the frames we draw by using these walls, what insures that they will persist?

2a.

Equality based on respect, when was that achieved between the green-eyed cat and his trainer?

How long after the end of love did they taste the consolation of an abiding friendship?

This is when I felt the need to invoke that ancient tale. Achieving balance among the elements of an artwork created with the human hand is one measure of excellence of perennial concern to the artist. But in that particular tale, I sense another, and even a superior, concern: how to encourage the reader to sense the hope that the natural inequality between the creative work and its creator will be overcome one day. The sculpture in the tale, even as it pleases its creator and captures his heart, is still his property, his creation. The sculptor, even while wishing that the sculpture were alive, even when his wish is fulfilled, is still the master of the sculpture. But later? A sculpture that ceases to match its definition also ceases to be. Perhaps a type of equality—one that at least an outside observer can sense—is achieved between the artist and the artwork. How difficult most of us find learning that what we have come to call happiness does not have to mean deriving pleasure from overpowering the other or being overpowered! But as soon as we achieve this type of equality around us, among those we've come to consider as intractable, there comes a stirring, a rupture . . .

4.

Fear: our dirt we are most inclined to cover; our odor we must struggle to conceal.

1a.

Tales. Somewhere in the habitual flow
>   (we really can't say that even our few daily routines have become habitual; true, expecting certain basic events to recur—albeit roughly—seems to make life easier, but otherwise, this "habitual" has no justification)

somewhere in the habitual flow of life
>   (and we tend to rely more than we should on the image of life flowing through its ups and downs— we mustn't forget)

somewhere in the habitual flow of life a fairy tale is always born when this flow, when this fabric of habit is suddenly ripped apart.

For those who forget the purpose of knowledge, those who mistake their weakness for strength, those who let love turn stale, while they are busy ripping this fabric, fear stands in wait, on both sides of the walls we have raised.

1977

13.

*We can understand each other, yes,
but can explain ourselves only to ourselves.*
—*H. Hesse,* Demian

*N*obody writes the travel memoirs of a dead writer. I decided to share my recollections with him and write what
he couldn't write, what he couldn't tell anybody else.

If I were to write

that we had met months ago

that we had left each other two days ago with the intent to
meet again in that medieval town,

that we had decided to participate as opponents (because our
relationship relied so much on trials and tests) in this laughable,
allegedly traditional game that was half unearthed from the
dustbin of history and half fabricated for the sake of the tourists

I thought

I would have represented him or the bond between us truthfully, befitting its inner reality.

There were thoughts we wanted to express but were afraid:

thoughts, emotions masked beyond recognition, beyond understanding, by our fear, by our futile attempts to express them. Each had expected the other to understand him without words, in the heart of our silence.

To what extent was I successful in describing what I knew through his eyes? In transcribing reality, what we took as our reality, through his words, in his manner?

He was the tall, dark one. I am a historian, it's a fact. The rest of the story I mostly made up while he was writing by the large window overlooking this hillside town, sleeping in the bed to my left, or reading in the armchair between the table and the bed, turned away from the window.

The autumn that died there along with him still lingers here, as if the winter is held back somehow. But the iron-colored sea refuses to free my gaze.

While leaving the garden, had I thrown myself in front of the angry man who attacked him for causing the town's team to lose the game, he wouldn't have been run over by a car and killed. Neither would I have died then.

In the town cemetery, while soil was being poured over his body, I asked myself, "Which of us is me, which is the one being buried?" as I stared past the wall, at the iron-colored sea. I still haven't found the answer.

He stopped breathing in my arms. Now what's the good of living after him?

1977